ACTION-PACKED
PAGE-TURNER

SET IN THE
JUNGLES OF
PAPUA NEW GUINEA

MEET FINN, A FEARLESS
FREE RUNNER
AND STUNT DOUBLE

ANOTHER FAST-PACED THRILLER
FROM TAMSIN COOKE,
AUTHOR OF
THE SCARLET FILES

ARE YOU FEARLESS
ENOUGH TO BE A
STUNT DOUBLE?

REVENGE OF THE ROPEN

A RIO DINONI MOVIE
COMING SOON

FILM INSIDER

Novak on board for new Dinoni Blockbuster

Acclaimed director Agatha Novak has confirmed that she'll begin production on the latest in the Rio Dinoni franchise next month. The project is currently top secret but rumour has it that it will be partly set in the jungle and involve an intensive shoot in a remote and exotic location. Novak is known for her eccentric behaviour, and has attracted negative publicity in the past for her outbursts on set, so we'll be keeping an ear out for any gossip as the project develops.

Trailer Talk

To loving mums everywhere.
Especially to my fabulous mum and wonderful
mother in law who are sadly no longer with us

OXFORD
UNIVERSITY PRESS

Great Clarendon Street, Oxford, OX2 6DP

Oxford University Press is a department of the University of Oxford.
It furthers the University's objective of excellence in research, scholarship,
and education by publishing worldwide. Oxford is a registered trade mark of
Oxford University Press in the UK and in certain other countries

Copyright © Tamsin Cooke 2017

The moral rights of the author have been asserted

Database right Oxford University Press (maker)

First published 2017

British Library Cataloguing in Publication Data
Data available

ISBN: 978-0-19-274982-6

1 3 5 7 9 10 8 6 4 2

Printed in Great Britain

Cover and inside illustration: abeadev/Shutterstock.com

STUNT DOUBLE

TAMSIN COOKE

OXFORD
UNIVERSITY PRESS

CHAPTER 1

Grabbing hold of another rock, I climb higher.

'Are you sure we should be doing this?' says Alex.

I glance down—he's about a metre behind—and below him, our tents look tiny. 'We've come this far. We can't give up now.'

'But the warnings were there for a reason,' says Alex.

'Exactly. We need to find out what they are.' The warning signs telling everyone not to climb the mountain were an invitation to me.

'Maybe we should go back,' says Alex.

'If you want to go back, feel free, but I'm going to find out what's up there.'

I climb higher, and smile to myself when I hear my younger brother's feet scuff the stones. He's following; I knew he would. The last part is steeper, and by the time I reach the top, I'm trying to catch my breath. I stare around, and my shoulders slump.

'It's a quarry,' says Alex, joining me.

'Why couldn't the signs have just said that?'

I'm not sure what I expected, but something better than this. The top of the mountain is relatively flat, with a cavernous hole dug out of its centre. There are no workmen, but the mountain is littered with cranes, diggers, and . . . military tanks?

'Let's go. This place gives me the creeps,' says Alex.

'Why are there tanks here?'

I hurry over to the nearest one, when the ground shakes. A deep rumble reverberates from the bottom of the pit.

'What's that?' yelps Alex.

I shrug. Forgetting the tanks, I creep towards the edge of the hole.

'I want to go back.'

'We will in a minute. Come and look.'

Alex drags his feet until he's beside me, and together we peer into the dark pit. I can't make out the bottom.

'How deep do you reckon it is?' I ask, when there's another rumble.

The ground jerks. I grab for Alex's hand, but the rock crumbles beneath him. His body drops, scraping against the stones. Screaming, he disappears into the hole.

'Alex!' I shout. I can't even see the top of his head.

'What are you doing here?'

I spin around to find five men dressed in protective gear, looking like scientists working on deadly diseases, not workmen.

'Get away from the edge,' one of them hisses, waving violently.

'I can't. My brother's down there. The ground gave way.' The words catch in my throat. Peering back into the darkness, I yell, 'Alex, are you all right?'

I hear footsteps, before a hand clamps around my mouth.

'Don't shout. You'll wake it up,' whispers a voice in my ear.

It? There's something down there . . . with Alex?

'We'll get your brother out but you need to step away from the edge and you need to be quiet. Do you understand?' says the man.

I nod and he lowers his hand. We shuffle backwards.

'We need a crane,' he says, and the others start moving.

'What should I do?' I ask.

'Stay out the way.'

The rock rumbles again. Then I hear a squawk—high-pitched, dripping with evil.

The man curses under his breath and shakes his head. 'It's awake. We've got to wait.'

'But my brother?'

'Shouldn't have been anywhere near here.'

My chest tightens. *It's my fault.* 'Can't you at least try?'

'I'm not risking the lives of my men.'

He takes my hand and tries to pull me away, but my feet remain rooted to the ground. My heart stops. On the spot where Alex disappeared, fingers grab onto the edge of the stone.

'Look,' I yell.

Two heads appear. One is my brother's with blood dripping from a cut; the other belongs to a boy about my age. He's carrying Alex on his back.

I leap towards them when the boy shouts, 'Stay where you are. The ground isn't stable.'

Feeling helpless, I watch the boy drag the pair of them over the edge. In a softer voice he says, 'You can let go now.'

Alex's arms fall away from his neck, and I drop to my knees beside my brother. 'I'm so sorry,' I whisper, trying to wipe the blood from his face.

Alex gives me a feeble smile.

I turn to the other boy. 'Thank you.'

'Not a problem,' he says, climbing to his feet. 'We should get out of here.'

The men dressed in protective clothing step closer.

'Who are you?' says the one who put his hand over my mouth. 'And what were you doing in my mountain?'

The boy brushes his hand through his dark hair, and

4

grins wickedly. 'The name's Rio Dinoni. And you know exactly why I'm here.'

'Cut!' The Assistant Director's voice rings out.

CHAPTER 2

The cameras stop rolling.

I try to bite back my grin. It's the first time I've ever spoken in a film, and I remembered my motivation, cues, and lines. We're inside a massive film studio, once an aeroplane hangar. One entire wall is covered in a green screen, ready for background scenery to be added later. The mountain is man-made with trees, rocks, patches of grass. It's at least twenty metres tall and thirty wide, but they'll make it appear even bigger with camera angles.

I hold out my hand and Alex (real name Joe) takes it. Pulling him up, I say, 'You were great.'

'Thanks bruv,' he says, his eyes sparkling.

I smile at his choice of words. He's not really my brother.

The AD, the assistant director, strides across the mountain. 'Great first take everyone.'

'Were me and Finn all right?' asks Joe.

I roll my eyes, as if the question is embarrassing, but I wait anxiously for the AD's reply.

'You were great, both of you,' he says.

Yes!!!!

Rio clears his throat or should I say Blake Saunders, the star of the Rio Dinoni franchise. The two previous Dinoni films were massive blockbusters. Blake rubs his neck, frowning.

'Is there a problem?' says the AD.

'Not a problem exactly,' says Blake, in his lazy voice, and for the first time since the cameras stopped rolling, he looks at me. 'You both *were* great, but I'm just not feeling it. Wouldn't it be better if there was an older sister rather than an older brother?'

He might as well have punched me in the face. I glance at the AD. *Ignore him.*

'Why do you say that?' says the AD.

'I just don't think this is the sort of boy who would stand back and let others save his brother. He'd fling himself into the pit. He'd scramble down that mountain.'

My insides groan. The thing is, Blake has a point. When I first read the script I thought the same. 'What if . . . what if I do just that? What if I leap into the pit, but

Rio has to rescue us both because it goes wrong?'

Blake smiles apologetically, and rubs his neck again. 'I'm sore enough with only Alex. I couldn't carry you too.'

Scratching his chin, the AD looks me up and down, and I almost see the cogs turning in his brain. 'If we had a girl, she could swoon over Rio, fall in love.'

'I could swoon,' I say.

The AD raises his eyebrow. 'I'm sure you could, but Rio would date a girl.'

My insides groan even more. My spoken lines are disappearing fast. 'What if I were injured? I had a crutch, so I couldn't rescue Alex.'

'If you had a crutch, I don't think you'd be climbing the mountain in the first place,' says Blake. 'Listen AD, you're the boss. I was only trying to help, make it more authentic.'

Blake's just said the magic word. Novak, the main director, is desperate for this film to be authentic.

The AD nods decisively and I know my role is gone. 'We'll find an older sister. Blake, do you need a stunt actor to carry Alex up the mountain for the next take?'

'I was hoping you were going to suggest that,' says Blake.

'All right then everyone,' shouts the AD, clapping his hands. 'We'll break for lunch, and afterwards redo the scene with an older sister.' Then he turns to me. 'Don't worry, you'll still get paid and a meal.'

That's not the point! Okay it is a point, we need the

money; but not the main point. I auditioned for this role. It's mine.

The crew and actors head down the makeshift mountain, but my feet refuse to budge. As Blake turns, his eyes hit mine and his lips twitch. My muscles tense. That little . . . He did it on purpose. Blake found a way for me to lose my lines. I glare back at him, and he winks before hurrying to join the others. Apart from him, no one else seems to notice that I stay where I am. I watch the actors and crew reach the bottom of the mountain, and head out of the hangar. The door slams behind them, leaving me alone.

For a moment, I kick loose stones, imagining each one to be Blake's head. Then I wander over to the edge of the deep pit. Blake's right. I would scramble inside and rescue Alex. I snort. I certainly wouldn't need a stunt actor to pick him up. Joe is eleven years old and weighs hardly anything. I leap over the edge onto a narrow ridge where Joe and Blake perch, just out of reach of the camera lens. I snort even louder. They could have gone deeper. Even though the walls are steep, there are rocks jutting out all over the place. Before I know it, I'm flying through the hole, landing knees bent on different ridges. Using my hands, I push off the wall and bounce from ledge to ledge. I forget about Blake. I forget about losing my lines.

The ceiling of the hangar becomes only a circle above, the rest hidden by walls of the mountain. I head to the bottom of the quarry, when I spot the black shape of a creature resting on the floor. Dangling from a rock, I stare at the metal prop. It's the Ropen—a mythological beast supposed to look like a pterodactyl about twice my size. I swing to the ground, careful not to touch it.

'Who are you?'

Startled, I jump backwards, my foot landing on the Ropen's claw. I hear a clink and feel the metal snap beneath me.

'What are you doing on my set?'

My stomach drops. Her 'what' sounds like 'vot'.

I stare in horror at Agatha Novak, the famous eccentric director. Not only am I trespassing, I've broken her precious monster.

CHAPTER

3

Novak's standing in front of a closed door cut into the mountainside. How long has she been down here?

'Come closer,' she says.

I don't move, I can't move. I'm obscuring the claw I've just snapped.

'Come closer,' she repeats, sharper this time.

Betting she's never disobeyed, I shuffle towards her when I feel a jolt of surprise. I heard she was short, but not this short. She comes up to my chest, her brown hair in a perfect bun.

'I'm sorr—'

'Name,' she cuts in.

Should I make one up? But if she finds out, I'll be in even more trouble. Covering my mouth with my hand, I cough, 'Finn.'

'What did you say?' she says, her voice thick with an Eastern European accent. She sounds like a Bond villain.

'Finn,' I cough again, when her phone rings.

'I have to get this.' She lifts her forefinger into the air, before adding, 'Stay.'

I'm not a dog! But I don't move. And if she says, 'sit,' I'll probably drop to the floor.

'Have you seen it?' Novak demands down the phone. 'So *you* haven't seen it? Someone else has . . . You know the rules . . . Rumours mean nothing.' She glares at me. Then turns her back, and starts speaking in a language I don't understand.

Part of me wishes she'd get it over and done with; tell me never to step foot on a film set again. Her voice grows louder, more agitated. She still has her back to me . . .

What am I waiting for?

Heart pounding, I inch backwards. Keeping my eyes fixed on her, I feel around the metal Ropen until it's standing between us. As quietly as I can, I grab a stone jutting out of the wall and slink up the inside of the mountain. My feet scuff the rock, and I wince every time I kick a stone off a ledge, but Novak doesn't seem to notice. She's yelling into her phone now.

I reach the perch where Blake and Joe hid, and pull myself over the top. I half scramble, half slide down the mountainside, before racing across the hangar. Slipping outside, I lean against the building. I catch my breath for a second, then join the main road that runs through the studio block. Walking quickly, I pass hangars and buildings, each housing different sets for the film. Novak booked the entire compound for the latest Rio Dinoni movie—*The Ropen's Revenge*. Nothing else is being filmed here.

I pass the canteen, when I hear, 'Finn, thank goodness.'

Turning around, I see my minder run towards me. *Oh my days!* I forgot about her. Everyone under sixteen must have an adult guardian with them. Film rules. My minder is twenty-five, blonde, brown-eyed, and right now, looking angry.

'Where have you been? You were supposed to be here twenty minutes ago,' says Selina.

'I got held up.'

'Doing what?'

'Filming.'

She doesn't look convinced, but she says, 'Well, you're here now. Let's get some lunch.'

I glance over my shoulder, looking out for Novak. 'Actually I don't want any. I've finished for the day, so I'm going to eat at home.'

Selina's eyes narrow. 'You should eat here.'

'I'm not hungry,' I lie. 'I thought you'd be happy. You get to finish early.'

She bites her lip. 'I tell you what. How about you eat in the canteen now, and I'll let you go home on your own? I'll only chaperone you to the studio exit.'

'Really?' Normally she hand delivers me to Mum as if I'm a baby. That's part of her contract. As I'm fourteen years old, it's humiliating.

'If you agree, I'll bend the rules a little,' she says.

'It's a deal.' If Novak comes in, I'll duck under a table or something.

Selina's face breaks into a grin, and she grabs hold of my arm. She pushes me through the door of the canteen, and I can't believe how busy it is. Actors, camera crew, grips, extras—they're all still here. Normally they grab a plate of food and eat in their designated green rooms. Actors stick together. Lighting stick together. But now they're standing, chatting, and holding plates.

Then I see why, and I also get why Selina wanted to come in here so badly. In the far corner of the room, surrounded by bodyguards and groupies, is Marcus Saunders. Blake's dad. More importantly, Hollywood royalty. Everything he stars in becomes a mega-blockbuster, and he has won almost every award possible. Everyone fancies him—even my mum.

'I'm going to get some food,' I tell Selina.

'Good idea,' she says, fluffing her blond bob, not taking her eyes off Marcus.

There are only extras left in the food queue. Technically I'm an actor—I auditioned and had lines—so

14

I should jump to the front. But having been the one always letting others go before me, I can't do it. So I join the end of the queue, behind two girls.

'I can't believe I'm going to get the chance to speak. First time I'm an extra and I'm talking,' says one of the girls, clasping her hands to her face. 'I get to climb a mountain. And swoon over Blake.'

'You do that anyway,' says the other girl, and they burst out laughing.

Seriously? Someone, somewhere must really hate me. I'm standing behind the girl who has my part. I should have pushed to the front after all.

'Blake is such a great actor,' she says.

'He's the best,' adds her friend.

I should keep quiet. I can't. 'You know Blake only got the role because of who his dad is,' I hiss quietly, not wanting Saunders Senior to overhear.

The girls look horrified. Role Stealer (okay—I know it's not technically her fault) folds her arms. 'That's not true. He went to seven auditions and beat 8,000 boys for this role. I read all about it on the Internet. It's got nothing to do with his dad.'

I snort.

'I think someone's jealous,' says the other girl.

'Jealous? Why would I be jealous of someone who can't even carry an eleven-year-old or scale down the inside of a mountain?'

'What are you talking about?' says Role Stealer.

'You'll find out.'

We move further up the queue, beside a table full of baguettes, biscuits, and more importantly, three doughnuts. The girls grab one each. I lean across, reaching for the third, when—

'Girls,' drawls a voice, and Blake is suddenly by my side. 'You don't mind do you?' He pushes in front and grabs the last doughnut.

'Didn't you want that?' says Role Stealer, looking at me.

'Oh he won't mind, will you *erm* . . . what's your name?' says Blake.

'Finn,' I mutter.

'You don't mind do you, Finn?' He takes a bite and winks. 'Got to go—I'm needed on set.'

I watch him saunter through the crowd, my fists clenching. *Will I ever be needed on set?*

'Oh my God, he winked at you,' squeals one of the girls. 'He actually winked at you.'

'He took the last doughnut,' I say.

'And he asked you your name. How many other actors would do that?' says Role Stealer.

They start discussing everything perfect about Blake, and through gritted teeth, I suck in breath. I could tell them a thing or two about Saunders Junior—how he really knows my name. We've known each other for four years, and he's hated me for three!

CHAPTER 4

I stand in front of my terraced house, my heart sinking. Could this day get any worse? I lost my role; the buses took forever to get through London, and now this. Balloons dangle from the drainpipe. Some bob up and down in the wind but others have popped, just shrivelled rubber floating in the air. I prefer those.

'Is it your birthday?' says Mr Darzi, my neighbour, walking past.

I shake my head.

'Then what are the balloons for?'

'I'm not sure,' I lie.

I wait until he turns the corner, then put my key in the lock. The door opens before I have a chance to twist it.

'Finn, you're early. Where's Selina?' says Mum, looking behind me.

'I left her at the end of the road.' Technically that isn't a lie. I don't say which road.

'So how's my superstar?' she asks, and I bundle her in the house, hoping no one heard. 'Did you see the balloons?'

'Yeah. They're great.'

'We need to take another picture of you, add it to our hall of fame.'

I glance at the photos hanging on the wall in our hallway, a line of them, starting with Mum from seventeen years ago. She's on different film sets in the first few, then there's a picture of her in the park with a large belly. I'm a baby in her arms in the next one. The rest are only of me—either school photos or each time I've been an extra in a film.

'We'll do it tomorrow,' I say.

'It's got to be today, but I've got something to show you first.' She ushers me into the lounge where a massive homemade banner covers the back wall. FINN'S FIRST WORDS.

'You make me sound like a baby.'

'You'll always be my baby,' she says, pinching my cheek with her thumb and finger. 'Did you remember your lines?'

'I only had seventeen.'

'Seventeen is more than none.'

Don't remind me!

Mum's eyes sparkle. 'Was Novak there? Did she hear?'

'She wasn't there when I did my bit.'

'But did you meet her?'

'Yeah.'

'Did she speak to you?'

'Yeah.'

'Did she talk to anyone else?'

'Not while I was there.' *There was no one else—thank God.*

'Novak doesn't just speak to anyone,' says Mum.

I can just imagine the conversations she'll be having in the hairdressers tomorrow: 'Novak chose Finn out of all the other actors to talk to. She's already singled him out. It's not surprising really. It's in his blood. Did I ever tell you about the time I . . . '

Should I tell her what happened? But she looks so happy.

'Listen Mum, I'm really tired. Do you mind if I go lie down?'

'But I thought we could order pizza to celebrate.'

'Can we afford it?'

She shakes her head. 'Don't you worry about the money. I'm the grown up—that's my job.'

I stare at Mum's platinum curls, false eyelashes, and excited pink cheeks. Exactly who is the grown-up?

'I've got homework.'

'Don't worry about that. School aren't going to care when they realize what you've been doing.'

*

'Do you think being in a film is an excuse?' demands Mr Willis.

This is the third time I've been asked that question, and it's only the second lesson.

'A little?' I say hopefully.

'Not one iota.' His eyes flash. 'Homework is set for a reason, and I'd like you to think about that reason during detention after school on Thursday.'

'Thursday?' I bounce on the balls of my feet. 'Would it be possible if I did it another day? It's just I have an exam.'

'In what?'

'In something,' I say, vaguely.

Mr Willis folds his arms and looks at me, obviously waiting for an answer. He'll be waiting a long time.

'Karate,' shouts Sam from the back of the room.

Okay—he won't be waiting that long. *But Sam, don't say anything else!* I shoot my best friend a look across the class.

'If he passes, he's going to be a black belt,' adds Sam.

What part of 'don't tell anyone' did he not understand? Murmurs are already spreading around the room.

'Black belt—impressive,' says Mr Willis. 'So you're in films, can act. I know you do free running. Is there anything you can't do?'

'Homework,' shouts Sam.

The class burst out laughing, and I try not to snigger.

Mr Willis's lips twitch. 'Oh sit down. You can have your detention on Friday.'

'Thanks Sir,' I say. Then pause. *Am I honestly thanking him for a detention?*

I start to walk to my seat, when Melinda, who doesn't normally notice I'm alive, clasps my arm.

'What's it like being in a Dinoni film?' she asks, looking at me in . . . adoration . . .

Whoa, this is new.

'It's all right,' I say casually, while my insides seem to jump.

'Did you meet Blake Saunders? Was he as lovely as everyone says he is? Can you get me his autograph?'

'Ooh—and me,' says Carla, sitting next to her.

There's a chorus of demands for Blake's autograph from every girl in the room, and my insides sink.

'Oh for goodness sake Finn, sit down,' snaps Mr Willis.

I fall into my seat beside Sam.

He clasps his hands together and bats his eyelids. 'Oh please get me Blake's autograph. I just love him!'

'Shut up. Or I'll practise some of my karate moves on you.'

*

Girls continue coming up to me all morning. They ask me the strangest questions. *Did I talk to Blake? What*

21

did he eat? What's his favourite colour, band, girl's name? What did he smell like? Thank God I never told anyone about me and Blake when I moved to this school two years ago.

At lunchtime, I grab a baguette and aim for the wall behind the school where no one else seems to go.

'Why don't you make something up?' says Sam. 'Say you and Blake are best friends. I reckon one of the girls would go out with you. You take Melinda. I'll ask Carla.'

I rip off a bit of baguette, wishing it were Sam's head.

'We could tell them what the film's about. Impress them,' he says.

'You don't know what it's about. It's top secret.'

'Yeah, I do,' says Sam, crisps spraying from his mouth. 'It's about a giant rodent who's got this bright blue stuff on his underbelly that helps him live forever. Rio needs to get some of it to stop his uncle from dying.'

I stare at my friend without blinking. Apart from getting the Ropen mixed with a rodent, he's pretty much on the money. How could he possibly know this?

Sam grins smugly. Then deepens his tone as if he's a voice-over actor on a movie trailer. 'In the depths of the jungle, the rodent's been captured by an evil tribe, desperate for the blue stuff themselves. Then out of nowhere, the rodent's mate appears, ready to exact revenge. What happens when our hero Rio Dinoni gets caught in the middle? Dun, dun, dunnnnnnn . . .'

Bloody Hell!

'I'm right, aren't I?' says Sam, his voice back to normal. He shoves another crisp in his mouth.

'No! Where did you hear that anyway?'

'Your mum told my mum at the salon yesterday, when she cut her hair.'

What????

I'm not even supposed to know the whole plot and I was in the film. But the girl from the costume department was showing off on set. Then I showed off to Mum . . . who showed off to Sam's mum . . . Oh God!

'Don't worry. I won't tell anyone,' says Sam.

'It's not even what it's about,' I say as casually as I can.

'Yeah right!' Then his eyes widen. 'No way. Don't tell me he wants Blake's autograph too.'

I turn to see where Sam's looking and I stiffen. Oli and his three minions from year ten are heading straight for us. I'm surprised they're in school. Normally they skip it.

'So you're a black belt?' says Oli, and even from over here, I see the glint in his eyes.

'Don't say a thing,' I hiss out of the corner of my mouth to Sam. Then louder, I say, 'No.'

'Everyone says you are,' says Oli, walking closer.

'Then everyone's wrong.'

'I reckon I could beat you.'

'I reckon you could too.'

'No, you couldn't,' says Sam, standing up. 'Finn might not be a black belt now but he will be on Thursday.'

I could kill him.

Oli's lip curls. 'You messing with me? Think you're clever?'

'No, I just don't want to fight,' I say, not sure who to glare at more; Oli or Sam.

'What? Scared you'll hurt me?' His voice drips with contempt.

I take a deep breath. I've had enough karate lectures to know this is a lose–lose situation. 'Sam, let's get out of here,' I say, jumping off the wall.

I should have known it was coming. A fist slams into the side of my head.

CHAPTER 5

I wince, the pain shooting through me.

'Not his face,' yelps Sam. 'He's in a film.'

Sam!

'Not his face, not his face,' jeer Oli's friends.

This time I sense the fist approach, and leap out the way. Oli punches with his other arm, straight for the gut. I guess I have no choice. Spinning around, I lift my leg and kick Oli. He falls sideways, but jumps back up and lunges. Spiralling around, I see one of Oli's minions leering. *Great!* It's going to be four against one. They pile in. I'd like to say my karate training kicked in. In all honesty, I lunge desperately—kicking one, jabbing another.

Out of the corner of my eye, I see Sam jumping in too. Oli aims for him. At the same time a fist slams into my jaw. I shake my head, trying to shake away the pain. Sam's being pummelled. I bend down and kick my leg upwards, smashing all my weight into Oli's chin. He crashes backwards.

'Stop!' roars a familiar voice.

As if in slow motion, we turn to Mr Willis, his face puce with anger. 'Get away from each other.'

We break apart.

'Who started it?'

No one says a thing. For once Sam keeps his mouth shut.

'Right then. You're all in detention with me after school today.'

'You've got to give us 24 hours' notice,' says Oli.

'Not for fighting I don't. But we can take it up with the police if you'd rather?'

'Detention today is fine,' says Oli.

'All of you in my form room at 3.30 sharp. I'm calling your parents now.'

Oh no! Mum tolerates not doing homework. Violence is something completely different.

*

Two and a half hours later, we're sitting in Mr Willis's form room. Oli shoots me looks and I don't have to be a mind-reader to understand them. He wants a rematch.

Why didn't I just let him win? And why did Sam have to tell the class I do karate? Some stupid muppet always wants a fight to prove themselves.

I squirm in my seat. The mobile phone in my pocket keeps vibrating, but there's no way I can answer it under Mr Willis's glare.

There's a knock on the door.

'Come in,' snaps Mr Willis.

The door opens and the school secretary walks in, holding a phone.

'Finn has an urgent call from his mother,' she says.

Without waiting for permission, I leap from my chair and grab the phone. 'What is it? What's happened?'

'Finn, you have to come home straight away,' says Mum.

'Is something wrong?'

'No,' says Mum, but her voice is quivering. 'Come home now.'

'I can't. I'm in detention.'

Mr Willis stares at me, his eyes narrowing to flints.

'Let me speak to your teacher,' says Mum.

'She wants to talk to you,' I say, handing him the phone.

'Is it a matter of life and death?' Mr Willis asks her, coldly. 'Then he is staying here. I will not tolerate fighting under any circumstances, especially from someone who is a black belt.'

He hangs up and I trudge back to my chair. What did Mum want? What could have been so urgent?

'Aww, did Mummy not get you out of detention?' says Oli.

'Silence!' shouts Mr Willis.

Five minutes later the door bursts open. No knock. Mr Willis opens his mouth to shout, but no sound comes out. No sound comes out of my mouth either.

Novak is striding into the room.

CHAPTER 6

Considering Novak is so small, she dominates the room. 'You,' she says, pointing at me.

My heart pounds. She's found out about the claw.

'It's such an honour to meet you,' says Mr Willis, holding out his hand.

'Hmmm,' she says, not even looking at him, and his arm drops awkwardly. 'Finn, why do you have detention?'

I take a deep breath. 'Fighting,' I say, giving her another reason to ban me from all future films.

'Boxing?' she asks.

'Karate.'

'Ah!'

I've no idea what 'Ah' means.

Her brow furrows and she claps her hands. 'But what are you still doing in your seat? You need to come with me.'

'Yes, Finn, what are you still doing in your seat?' says Mr Willis.

My eyes dart between the pair of them. Is this for real?

'Get up. Off you go,' says my teacher.

I leap up before either change their mind.

'What about us? Can we go?' says Oli.

'Do you have a famous director after you?' says Mr Willis.

'No.'

'Then you are staying here.'

I smile apologetically to Sam, who stares at me with his mouth open, for once lost for words. Leaving the room, the boys' glares burn the back of my head. Mr Willis has given them another reason to want to kill me, but that's tomorrow's problem. Right now I've got to work out how to pay for the broken claw. It must have cost a fortune if Novak came all the way over here to see me.

'Take me to the car park,' she orders.

I lead her through the school and soon we're standing on tarmac. Not many cars are here now, and certainly no limo. She heads over to a two-seater sports car, and opens the driver's door.

'Get in,' she says.

'Don't you have a driver?'

'I do not trust anyone else with my films, why would I trust them with my life?'

I climb in. Before my door is even shut, Novak swerves out of the car park. I manage to slam it, as she hurtles down the road. Snapping my seatbelt into place, I stare in horror at the speedometer. She turns a corner and floors the accelerator.

'The lights are red!' I yell.

'I'm colour blind,' she replies, driving faster.

We speed through the traffic lights, other cars veering out the way, their horns blaring.

'You went through a red light.'

'You're still alive,' she says calmly.

I don't know how! She spins down a road, but she's on the wrong side.

'We drive on the left here,' I yell, grabbing the steering wheel, yanking the car left just as a motorbike appears.

Novak turns to look at me, her eyes on fire.

'The road,' I yelp. 'Look at the road.'

She sniffs, and coolly faces the front. 'If you touch my steering wheel again, I will make you get out and walk.'

'I'll walk now.'

'You are a funny boy,' she says, turning left again, and suddenly I realize we're nearing my house.

'You know where I live?'

'I looked it up on a map. I have a very good sense of direction.'

She parks the car in our street. Literally. She pulls up

outside our house, and parks the car in the middle of the road.

'You can't leave it here, other people need to get past.'

'They will be fine,' she says. 'But Finn, who do you think you are, giving me orders? Now get out, your mama is waiting.'

I scramble out of the car. Would it be rude to kiss the ground?

Mum opens the door before we reach the pavement, and a man towers behind her, so massive he makes the Incredible Hulk look like one of the seven dwarves. He's dressed in black, and wearing an earpiece. Oh no. Don't tell me he's the secret police coming for the claw.

'My bodyguard,' explains Novak. 'There wasn't enough room for him in the car when I came to get you.'

Lucky him!

My legs are still shaking as I follow Mum into the lounge. She's obviously making an effort. There are chocolate biscuits, and teacups, and saucers on a tray. No mugs in sight. The four of us fill the space, and for the first time this room seems tiny and shabby. I notice a stain on the carpet. What the hell is wrong with me? This is my home. I don't—I won't—care what Novak thinks.

I squeeze next to Mum on the sofa, while Novak sits in an armchair on the other side of the coffee table, her bodyguard standing behind. The cup rattles in the saucer as Mum pours tea for Novak. She's more nervous than me.

'I'll do it,' I say, taking it from her.

'Would you like a biscuit?' says Mum, offering Novak the plate.

Novak peers at them before wrinkling her nose. 'No.'

Hurt flashes across Mum's face, and I fight the urge to fling the tea over Novak's head.

'I imagine you are wondering why I'm here,' says Novak, after a long sip.

'I was wondering,' says Mum, in her best telephone voice.

'I saw your son on set,' says Novak.

'I knew it.' Mum's face breaks into a giant grin. 'I always knew Finn would be discovered.'

'Mum, no—'

It's too late. A raging Ropen would be helpless against her.

'Finn was the first winner of the Saunders scholarship,' she says.

'The Marcus Saunders scholarship?' Novak peers at me with renewed interest.

Marcus Saunders set up the scholarship four years ago to help children from deprived areas learn drama.

'It's such an accomplishment,' says Mum. 'You have to pass rigorous tests, and Saunders only chooses the best children, the ones with the greatest potential.'

Kill me now! 'Mum, I don't think Novak is here because of my great potential.'

'You know Blake then?' says Novak, staring at me curiously.

'Yeah, I—'

'They went to drama club together,' says Mum. 'Then Blake got the role of Rio, and I don't think Finn has seen much of him since then. Until your film that is.'

'Interesting,' says Novak.

'It is interesting because Finn won the scholarship and Blake didn't,' says Mum.

Let me curl up and die. 'Well his dad couldn't have awarded his own son the scholarship, could he? Especially when he's—you know—loaded,' I turn to Novak. 'Did I break something?'

'Yes, you did.'

The teacup slips from Mum's hand, but somehow doesn't break. Scooping it off the floor, she says, 'You broke something? You never said.' Her face pales and I know she's thinking about the money.

'I can repay it,' I say.

'It is over a thousand pounds,' says Novak.

How much??? Mum gasps.

'It was just a foot,' I whisper.

'An electronic foot that moved. It used to anyway,' says Novak. 'But I am not here about the claw. That is not my concern. You are.'

CHAPTER

7

'What were you doing on my mountain?' says Novak.

'Climbing it.'

'No, you weren't. You were skipping, leaping, diving about.'

'It's called free running.'

'Oh Finn, you were playing on set?' Mum looks horrified.

Leaning back in the armchair, Novak says, 'In the olden days when I first started, cinematography was so much more authentic. Real. I detest CGI but it is something I have to use.' She waves her hand, dismissively. 'My actors aren't able to do their own stunts.

35

It's in their contract. They could hurt themselves and set back the timing of the film. Blake is only fourteen so he can hardly do anything. He also chooses to do nothing. He is, however, integral to the Dinoni franchise, and girls seem to love him.'

'Girls love my Finn too,' says Mum.

The bodyguard snorts, and I shoot Mum a look.

'Seeing you climb means you are not afraid of heights. You are very physical. And I know you do not get car sick,' says Novak.

'Oh! Your driving was a test,' I say.

'No,' she says with a frown. 'My driving was perfect. I just know this fact from your CV.' She pauses. 'You have blue eyes like Blake, are about the same height. A little more muscly I think, but with the right hair, you could pass off as him.'

'Why would I want to do that?'

'Because I want you to be his stunt double.'

I stare at her in amazement.

'We use women to carry out stunts for boys. Even if there is a man short enough, he is too broad. Too muscular. Women are the right height and often slender, but they are curvy—have hips and thighs. I have to take every shot from a wide angled camera. But you—you would be good.'

'Is this even legal?' says Mum.

My eyes dart to her in surprise. I thought she'd be signing the contract by now.

'As long as no lawyers hear about it, it is fine,' says Novak.

'So not legal then?' says Mum.

'Bah!' says Novak. 'Finn will be paid incredibly well—the same wage as a grown-up stunt double. The claw he has broken will be forgotten. And he will be coming with us to Papua New Guinea.'

'I'll do it,' I say.

'But he won't get any recognition,' says Mum. 'Everyone will think it's Blake doing the stunts.'

'You're right. Not this time. We will have to keep him a secret from the world. But if he works hard and proves himself, maybe he will be the star of my next film.'

'Where do we sign?' says Mum, catching my eye, her toes beginning to tap up and down in excitement.

Novak beams, before pulling out the largest stack of papers I've ever seen. 'Just some forms,' she explains, as Mum grabs a pen off the coffee table.

'Don't you think we should read them first?' I ask.

'Oh, yes—yes, of course,' says Mum, putting the pen down.

'When would I start?'

'Ideally it would be tomorrow,' says Novak. 'But you have school. Plus it is a hard first stunt. I think we should ease you in gently.'

I lean forward. 'I don't mind starting tomorrow. Mum, do you think you could get me out of school?'

'I'll get you permission,' she says.

'Then here is the script. Your parts are highlighted,' says Novak, pulling out a second wad of paper. She also brings out some DVDs. 'And this is your homework for tonight. Blake Saunders is in them. Watch him—see how he runs, climbs, so that you can mimic his movements, his mannerisms.' She stands up. 'Now we must be on our way. I shall send a car to pick you up as we need to start early.'

Send a car????

Mum and I walk Novak and her bodyguard outside. A crowd of neighbours circle her sports car.

'Hey Finn, do you know who left this?' demands Mr Darzi. 'It's a nuisance.'

'I did,' says Novak.

The crowd falls silent, their jaws dropping, and they part like the Red Sea as Novak strides towards the car.

'Would you like me to drive?' asks her bodyguard, opening the driver's door.

'No,' she says sharply.

The bodyguard's face pales and this time I snort loudly.

As Novak swerves away. Mr Darzi says, 'What were they doing at yours?'

'It's a secret,' says Mum, waltzing back into the house. Once the front door closes, she squeals, 'I always knew your free running and karate lessons would pay off. Finn, this could be your big break.'

I grin at her, then open my script. Glancing down at the action shot for tomorrow, my grin vanishes. *Seriously?* They can't expect me to do this . . . can they?

CHAPTER

8

F ive o'clock in the morning and I'm standing at one end of Tower Bridge in London. Conner, an Australian stuntman and my new minder, picked me up from my house. Luckily he drove like a normal human being—not like a stuntman in a car chase.

The whole area is cornered off. No cars or pedestrians are allowed, but crew are everywhere. There are cameras on jibs for sweeping shots, wires dangling from cranes, and boom poles for sound (microphones on the end of long rods).

'How are you feeling, Kid?' says Conner.

'All right,' I say, trying to sound braver than I feel.

The bridge is bigger than I remembered. There are

two horizontal walkways—one high, one low—fixed between two towers. We're on the lower walkway. It splits into two equal parts which rise like swinging doors to allow boats to pass. Novak is nearby, talking to a tall, thickset man whose neck is probably the size of my body.

'That's Alistair, stunt coordinator. Our boss,' says Conner.

'He doesn't look happy,' I say, which is a bit of an understatement. Alistair has a face like thunder, and when he spots me, it darkens even more.

'Him?' he shouts. 'That's a child!'

'He is more than capable,' says Novak.

'I could get into trouble over this,' says Alistair.

'You could also lose your job. How long have you been trying to work for me?'

A vein throbs on Alistair's forehead. 'Are you threatening me?'

'Threaten is such an ugly word. Give Finn a chance, let him prove himself. If he fails, then I fire him.'

Hey! What?

'What if he gets hurt?' says Alistair.

'He won't. You're here.'

Heading over, Novak smiles warmly, and I half expect her to ruffle my hair like Mum would. 'I know you can do it, Finn,' she says, before walking past me.

'If you have any sense, you'll fail,' spits Alistair. He throws something beige and covered in hooks at me. 'Put this on.'

'What is it?' I ask, catching it.

He rolls his eyes. 'If you were a real stunt double you'd know.' Without another word, he storms off in the same direction as Novak.

'Don't mind him,' says Conner. 'His girlfriend was supposed to be Rio's stunt double and he thought they'd be working together.' He taps the bundle I'm holding. 'It's a jerk vest. Put it on. It will save your life.'

I hold it out. It's a cloth harness that looks like a waistcoat with straps and buckles instead of buttons down the front. Hooks are positioned in various places, and there are two padded straps that look like they go between my legs and support my bum.

'Step into it,' says Conner.

I do as he says and he tightens the buckles, leaving me just enough room to breathe. Then he leads me over to a crane with wires dangling down.

'We hook you up to this rig. That way if you slip, you won't go far, the wires'll hold you in place.'

Conner connects the wires to hooks on my shoulders and back, and nods to the man operating the rig. Without warning I'm swept off the ground, swinging in the air like a puppet.

'A heads-up would have been nice,' I shout.

'Where's the fun in that?' says Conner, in between snorts of laughter, and I'm lowered back to the ground. 'We're going to practise twice, so you know exactly what you're doing, and the cameramen can work out the best angles to film you. After that, we'll do the real thing.'

I nod and try to look calm.

'Don't look so worried. We're here to help if it goes wrong.'

Obviously I don't look that calm.

'You know what to do? You read your script?'

'Yeah,' I say, but it comes out in a whisper. 'Yeah,' I say louder.

'Good. For the practice, we don't want you jumping off. Run to the top, then stop. We don't want you getting wet and cold for no reason.'

There's a grinding noise and very slowly, the bridge begins to lift; the two parts—the bascules—rising upward like wings. Then suddenly the hairs on the back of my neck shoot up as if someone's staring. Glancing over my shoulder, I see Alistair and Novak.

'Fail,' mouths Alistair.

Not helping!

Even though Novak smiles at me, her words fill my brain: 'If he fails, I'll fire him.'

I push these thoughts to the back of my mind. *I can do this. I have to.* Facing forward, I visualize everything I have to do. I work out where I'm going to run, where I'm going to put my feet. The bascules are now sloping over 45-degree angles, and each is about thirty metres high. Craning my neck, I look at the very top. *Whoa!*

'Are you ready?' says Conner.

I take a deep breath.

The AD shouts, 'Action.'

I dart under the archway of the first tower. If I don't get momentum, I'm going to slip back down. Racing as fast as I can, my trainers hit the rising floor. It's like running up a death slide that's getting steeper and steeper.

My feet stumble, but I feel the wires on my vest tighten, refusing to let me fall. Confidence surging, I scramble up the rest of the bascule, my hands grabbing onto the edge of the bridge. My body lies flat against the rising wing. Using all the strength in my arms, I heave myself up until I'm balanced on the ridge. Glancing down, ice showers my body. It's high. Far too high. Thank God for wires!

'Cut!'

The wires jerk, and I find myself flying back to the ground. Cheers erupt around me, but there's only one person's reaction I care about. My eyes fall on Novak and she's nodding. *Yes!!!* To the side of her, Alistair is shaking his head, but I don't care what he thinks.

'That was awesome,' yells Conner, running towards me. 'Ready to do it again?'

The second practice goes even better, and soon I'm bustled into a trailer where hair and make-up take place.

'You looked like you were enjoying yourself,' says the hairdresser, scraping my blond hair off my face.

'You saw me?'

'Yeah. We always watch the stunts. They're the most exciting parts.'

My chest expands.

'Was it scary?' she asks, picking up a wig.

'A bit,' I admit, and she laughs. 'It was like a roller-coaster ride. You're scared, but you know you're safe, or hope you are anyway.'

'Alistair wouldn't let anything happen to you,' she says, jabbing a pin into my head.

'Ow! Are those hair clips or staples?'

'I have to make sure your wig doesn't fall off.' She grabs my shoulders. 'Stop wriggling—should I use superglue?'

'Is that an option?'

'Hah!'

Make-up isn't much better. I don't know how girls cope with this stuff plastered to their face. The make-up artist's eyes are centimetres from mine, scrutinizing every centimetre of my skin.

'Perfect,' she says finally.

'And it only took half an hour,' I mutter.

'That's not long. Some actors have to stay for hours and hours.'

I try not to grin. She called me an actor.

'Ready to see yourself?' she says, holding up a mirror.

I stare into the glass. If I was in a cartoon, my eyes would pop out of my head, but this is no cartoon. This is a horror film. 'I look like Blake.'

'And my work here is done,' says the make-up artist, taking a small bow. 'You need to go to wardrobe next.'

I can hardly tear my eyes away from the mirror, when

a door opens and Novak steps inside. 'My goodness,' she says, her eyes widening. 'Stasia, you are remarkable.'

Stasia, the make-up artist, curtsies this time.

'But now, would you leave us please,' says Novak. 'I want a word with Finn in private.'

'Of course,' says Stasia, scurrying outside.

'Is everything okay?' I ask.

'Everything is almost perfect,' says Novak.

'Almost?'

'Finn, you know how I don't like CGI. Well I don't want to use it in your stunt. I don't want to have to use a computer to get rid of the wires. It seems fake.' She smiles maternally. 'I was thinking—you don't need to wear the jerk vest. For the real thing, why don't we leave out the wires?'

CHAPTER 9

Half an hour later, wearing a wetsuit under jeans and a t-shirt, I'm standing in my starting spot on the bridge.

Conner's brows shoot to the top of his head, and he starts patting me down. 'Where's your jerk vest? You're supposed to be wearing it under your t-shirt.'

'Novak didn't want me to wear it,' I say.

'Are you crazy? What if you slip back down?'

'Then I slip back down. It's not far.'

'It's thirty metres, and you're almost vertical.'

'It's fine,' I say, hoping he doesn't catch the quiver in my voice.

'Does Alistair know?'

I shrug.

Conner points a finger at me. 'Listen very carefully. I'm going to find Alistair, and I do not want you starting the stunt without me. Ignore cameramen, ignore directors. Do you understand?'

I nod, just as the bascules begin to rise.

Conner runs off the bridge and I close my eyes. I need to get Conner and his doubts out of my head. I need to get into character. Rio Dinoni wouldn't need a jerk vest. And I am Rio—running away from baddies. I can't let them catch me or the fate of the world is at stake.

With my eyes closed, the grinding of the bridge seems louder. I take deep breaths, and visualize the bascules growing steeper, the steps I have to make, then the jump.

Someone shouts, 'Action!'

My eyes flash open. Pumping my arms like Blake, I dart under the tower, and charge up the slope. Running as fast as I can, I think only of the top. I have to get up there. Thighs burning, my feet stumble and I slide backwards. *Nooo!* I pound my feet and arms even harder. I can't go back to the bottom. Sweat pouring down my back, I feel like I'm running on the spot. Almost crawling, somehow my fingers reach the ledge at the top, and I dangle down, my body flush against the vertical bridge. My toes scramble against the stone and I pull myself onto the edge. I perch, knees bent on top of it. In my mind, I hear the baddies chasing me. I look

47

at the opposite upended bascule. Rio's supposed to try to jump it, thinking he can make it.

I leap across, and following the script, plummet to the river. The water crashes over my head, and my body hurtles down. Bubbles of air explode from my mouth and nose, and the water soaks through my clothes, dragging me deeper.

Opening my eyes, I see nothing but cloud and silt. I claw through the water, and kick my legs, my lungs desperate for air. At last I break through the surface, and take giant gulps. The ladder on the other side of the river seems so far away. I swim for it, even though my clothes and trainers seem intent on pulling me down. My limbs begin to seize. Just two more strokes and I'm there. My fingers grasp the rung of the ladder and I drag myself upwards. The cold wind envelops me, and I start to shake. I reach the top and collapse on the side of the bank.

'Cut!'

Somehow I manage to stand. Blankets are thrown over me, and all I can hear are cheers and yelps of glee. I did it! I nailed it! I peek out of the blanket to find Conner glaring at me.

'What were you thinking? Did you not understand my instructions?'

My teeth chatter and I can't bring myself to speak.

'Finn, I was about to dive in and get you. I thought you were going to drown. And when you slipped on the bridge, I thought I'd be mopping up your brains.'

'Sorry,' I manage. 'Wh—where's Alistair?'

'He sent me. He didn't trust himself—said he wanted to murder you.'

I drop my head and Conner sighs.

'Listen, you did well, I grant you that. And you made it look real, but you should never do stunts without your stunt team present. You should have worn a jerk vest. I should fire you.'

'He was following my instructions,' says Novak.

I turn my head in surprise. I hadn't heard her approach. By the look on Conner's face, he hadn't either.

'And I am afraid you can't fire him, as I am firing you. No one questions my directions,' says Novak.

It's like I'm back in the water, unable to find air. Conner's mouth drops open. I'm vaguely aware of cheering still going on. They can't have heard.

'Finn, you did well,' says Novak. 'I knew you wouldn't let me down. Now, you need to do it again. One take is never enough.' Then she looks at me accusingly. 'You're wet. You need to start off dry.'

Something inside me snaps. 'I'm not doing it again.'

'What?'

I take a deep breath. 'I'm not doing it again unless you rehire Conner. He was looking out for me. He was doing his job. He shouldn't lose it.'

'Hey Kid, don't worry about—'

'No. You were worried about me. You shouldn't be fired for it.'

Under Novak's glare, my insides wither, and I realize what I've done. I've lost my job again.

Novak glances behind her, surveying the scene. 'It appears nobody heard your little outburst, Finn, otherwise you would be fired too.' Then she turns to Conner. 'The boy makes a good point. Okay, you are back on the team. But if you ever tell him to do something other than what I say, or you refuse to follow my order, you will be off my film set quicker than it takes a clapperboard to snap. There are plenty of people who would dream of doing your job. Do I make myself clear?'

'Yeah,' says Conner.

'Good. Now take him to hair and wardrobe. He needs a dry wig and clothes.'

'She must really like you,' says Conner, as we head back to the trailer. He pauses. 'Thanks, Kid.'

✳

Two hours later, we redo the shoot. Shivering in a blanket, I'm sitting cradling my knees, back on the bank. Not only are the crew cheering, but members of the public are hanging out of windows to watch. I feel a bit like a superstar. Keeping my hood over my head, so they can't see who I am, I lift my arm and wave. The cheers grow louder.

'You were awesome,' says an American voice.

I peer out and gasp, then try to look cool. Anna Morrow is standing in front of me. She's *the* rising star, playing Rio's girlfriend in this film.

'When they told me you were only fourteen, I couldn't believe it. You're really brave,' she adds.

'Or stupid!'

'That too,' she says, flicking her long blond hair.

I laugh, when a familiar voice drawls, 'Those stunts were impressive.'

For a moment I freeze. Was Blake Saunders actually being nice to me? Even though I'm numb with cold, I pull the blanket off my head a little, making sure it's Blake who's talking.

It *is* him.

His eyes widen and his lips pull back into a snarl. 'What are you doing here?'

'I'm your new stunt double.'

'Like hell you are! I'm seeing Novak about this. There's no way you're working on this film.'

As he storms off, Anna says, 'He really hates you.'

'The feeling's mutual.'

She grins. 'I think you and I are going to become great friends.'

'That's if I still have a job,' I say, pulling the hood back over my face.

'Why do you two hate each other anyway?'

I don't say anything. I've never told anyone, and I'm not about to now.

CHAPTER
10

Back in wardrobe, I put on my own dry clothes, scrub my face, mush up my hair, and glance in the mirror. *Yes!* Blake has vanished. Feeling like me again, I head outside, straight into the path of the AD. I haven't spoken to him since the day he took away my lines, and right now, he's looking sheepish. My heart sinks.

'Kid, I was looking for you.'

Now he's calling me Kid?

'Blake Saunders has been to see me,' he says.

I bet he has, but I don't say anything. I don't trust the words that want to come out of my mouth.

The AD clears his throat. 'It appears that you and

Blake have a little history. He doesn't seem that keen on working with you.'

I bite back a laugh. Talk about understatement!

'However, when I mentioned this fact to Novak, she didn't seem to care. She said losing you was not an option. You *will* remain as Blake's stunt double.'

'She did?'

'Yeah! She likes you,' he says, with undisguised surprise. 'So that puts me in a bit of a predicament. I can't get rid of Blake—he *is* the film. And I can't get rid of you.'

'You want me to resign?'

'No, no, you can't do that.' He clears his throat again. 'I spoke to Blake a second time and he is willing to work with you under one condition.'

Oh God!

'He wants you to be his PA. His Personal Assistant. You'll be like a secretary, carrying out his wishes.'

'I'll be his slave?'

'No.'

Yes! Blake wants to order me around; make my life hell.

The AD rolls onto the balls of his feet. 'I can't see another way around it, Kid. Would you help me out?'

What happens if I say no? But surely if I can jump off a bridge into the River Thames, I can do this. I mean—how bad can it be?

'Sure, I'll do it.'

The AD beams.

'If you stop calling me ki—'

'I HAVE PROOF!' screams a voice.

The AD and I spin around to see Novak charging towards us, waving her mobile in the air. Thrusting the phone under the AD's nose, I watch his eyes widen. He curses under his breath. I lean forward and try to peek at the image, but Novak snatches the phone back, cradling it to her chest.

'You were right,' whispers the AD.

'I know,' says Novak smugly. 'When are we going to Papua New Guinea?'

'In two weeks' time. It's all booked.'

'No, that's not acceptable. We go tomorrow.'

The AD and I glance at each other before looking back at Novak. My heart starts pounding. *Is that me as well? Will I be going?*

'Tomorrow. Are you joking?' he says.

'Have you ever heard me joke?' says Novak.

The AD scratches his chin. 'But everything and everyone is prepared for two weeks. We can't just expect—'

'We can,' she interrupts. 'The crew *will* make themselves available. I booked the hotel early just in case this happened. It's empty at the moment. And I'm sure you can find us a pair of aeroplanes. I hired you because you are someone who gets things done. Was I wrong?'

The AD gulps.

'Anything is possible if you are willing to pay. And

I am more than willing to pay. From what I've seen,' she adds, waving her phone, 'we will treble if not quadruple our profits.'

The AD nods. 'All right, I'm on it,' he says, striding away.

'Have you ever been to Papua New Guinea?' Novak asks me.

'I've never been on an aeroplane or abroad before.'

'Really? Then you, my boy, are about to have the adventure of a lifetime. Together we will discover the land of the Ropen.'

'Isn't the Ropen just a myth?'

She smiles, like she's hiding some great secret.

'But . . . but what about Mum?' I say suddenly. 'Will she let me go? I've got school and—'

'I've already spoken to your mama on the phone and she was more than happy to give permission. I explained how you will join Anna and Blake in their lessons to continue your education.'

'So . . . I'm really going?'

'Yes. Conner will take you home now. You need to pack.'

I want to jump up and down. I'm going abroad. I'm missing school, my karate exam, and detention. But as I search for Conner, something occurs to me. Novak spoke to my mum before speaking to the AD.

*

55

On the way home, I'm almost bouncing in my seat. This time tomorrow I'll be on an aeroplane.

'Is it normal to bring trips forward like this?' I ask.

'No,' says Conner. 'But Novak is . . . how should I put it . . . eccentric? This is the second time I've worked with her.'

Conner tells me about all the stunts he's done before, the countries he's visited, the films he's been in.

'Being a stunt double is the best job in the world. It's way better than being an actor. You get to have the most fun, without any of the pain of being famous. You can go to the supermarket and no one knows you; you don't get mobbed.'

'Wouldn't a little mobbing be nice?'

Conner laughs. 'No, it wouldn't. When you see what Blake has to put up with, you wouldn't want to swap places with him for the world.'

I'm not so sure, but I don't say anything. We pull up outside my house and to my horror, there are even more balloons dangling from the drainpipe.

'Is it your birthday?' says Conner.

I shake my head. 'Mum's proud of me.'

'Mums are great, aren't they?' says Conner with a grin. 'What about your dad? Is he proud too?'

'I don't know. He left when Mum was pregnant.'

'Aw Kid, I'm sorry,' says Conner, looking mortified.

'It doesn't bother me. If he's the sort of man who leaves when someone's pregnant, I don't want to know him.'

'I guess,' says Conner. 'And your mum more than makes up for him, doesn't she?'

'Unfortunately, yes.'

I climb out of the car and hurry to the front door, before Mum can appear. She'll probably start throwing confetti or have a marching band ready to announce my arrival.

'I'm home,' I shout, slamming the door behind me.

'Finn, come into the lounge,' she yells.

Oh no—what's going to be there this time?

MY SON THE SUPERSTAR is plastered on a banner across the wall. She's standing with a camera in her hand.

'You're going to Papua New Guinea,' she squeals.

'I know!' And with no one watching but Mum, I jump into the air.

'I couldn't believe it when Novak rang,' says Mum. 'She asked if you had a passport and I said no. So she sent someone over with forms and for photos. What it is to be rich and famous! How many other people could arrange a passport in less than 24 hours?'

Then it hits me. I'm leaving the country. I won't see Mum for—I don't know how long. I've never spent more than one night away from her. I hope she'll be okay. I hope I'll be okay too.

'Novak must really want you there,' says Mum.

'But why?'

'She's seen your potential. She can see what I've known all along.' Mum pauses. 'But she also asked me for a favour.'

'She did?'

'I know—imagine that! Novak wanting a favour from me.'

'What is it?'

Mum starts twisting a hooped earring, before blurting it out.

'Tell me you said no,' I say.

'What do you think? I can't refuse Agatha Novak.'

I step back. Mum's right—whatever Novak wants, she gets. But why does she have to want this?

CHAPTER 11

'Finn, are you up?' calls Mum through the bedroom door.

My eyes open blearily. Then I bolt upright. I'm not late am I? But when I glance at the clock, it's only 8.15, and Conner's not coming around until 10. I'm already packed.

'I'll be down in a bit,' I say, rolling over. It took me ages to get to sleep last night. My brain was far too busy.

'There are some girls downstairs. They want to see you,' says Mum.

Girls? They never come here.

She pops her head around the door. 'I think they want autographs. They have paper in their hands.'

59

'Really?' I say, sitting up. 'Sam must have told them about me. I texted him last night. Told him I wouldn't be at school for a while.'

Mum frowns. 'You didn't tell him you were a stunt double, did you?'

'No! I'm under contract,' I say, climbing out of bed. 'Will you get out, so I can get dressed?'

Mum closes the door and I sniff my armpits. Good—I don't stink. There's no time for a shower before I see the girls, whoever they are. I yank on my favourite shorts and t-shirt I'm wearing on the plane, and run down the stairs. I stop at the bottom, give myself a shake, then casually open the door. Melinda and Carla stand on the doorstep, pink paper in their hands.

'Girls,' I say, imitating Blake's lazy drawl.

They stare at me for a moment before they start giggling. Are they giggling at me or for me? My cheeks grow hot.

'I almost didn't recognize you,' says Carla.

'You've seen me out of uniform before, haven't you?' I say, scraping my hand through my hair, and suddenly I know. Mum's favour to Novak. I can't believe I forgot. My brain must have blocked it. 'The director wants some actors to look like Blake.'

'So you had to dye your hair?' says Carla.

'And have it cut?' says Melinda.

'Mum did it last night,' I say, wanting nothing more than to close the door and hide. Forever.

Melinda leans forward. 'You know—you do look a bit like Blake now.'

'That's what I'm afraid of.'

'It's a good thing.'

'Blake is still far better-looking,' says Carla, looking me up and down as if I'm a mannequin in a shop window.

'I know that,' says Melinda.

'He has a stronger jaw, and those eyes.'

'Oh those eyes.' And they start giggling again.

'You know I'm standing right here and can hear every word you're saying. Did you want something?'

Carla elbows Melinda.

'Finn,' says Melinda, pleadingly. 'I don't suppose you'd do us a favour?'

'As long as it doesn't have anything to do with my hair.'

'Will you get Blake Saunders' autograph for us? I've perfumed the paper.'

She holds out the pink sheets, and I slam the door in her face. I hear a gasp.

'That's your fault. You said he wasn't as good-looking as Blake.'

'He isn't.'

'I know that but—'

I don't bother listening to the rest of their conversation. I sprint upstairs and jump in the shower. Even though I wash my hair again and again, it remains just as black.

★

An hour later, Conner is at the door, and I'm ready—a beanie hat firmly attached to my head.

'You sure you've packed everything?' says Mum.

I nod.

'You have enough underpants?'

'Mum,' I groan, my face and neck feeling impossibly hot. 'Let's go,' I say to Conner.

He grabs my suitcase and says with a laugh, 'By the weight of this, you've packed enough underpants for a year.'

'Ha!'

Mum grabs hold of Conner's arm. 'You'll make sure he's looked after, won't you?'

'He's my minder. He'll be with me the whole time,' I say.

'Everyone will make sure Finn's fine,' says Conner. 'After all, he's one of Novak's favourites.'

Mum's eyes well up and she wraps her arms around me. 'Make me proud. But most importantly, enjoy yourself.'

'I will. I'll miss you,' I say, and she bursts into tears.

'I think we'd better go, or we'll miss the plane,' says Conner.

He puts my bag in the boot and I climb into the passenger seat. We leave Mum sobbing and waving on the pavement outside my house. I half expect her to run alongside our car, and now I feel a lump forming in my throat. I look out of the window, squeezing back tears.

'You'll be all right, Kid. So will your mum,' says Conner. 'Have I told you about all the gear I've got you? You are now the proud owner of a jerk vest and safety pads for almost every part of your body.' He peers at me out of the corner of his eyes. 'That's if you choose to wear them.'

Conner spends the rest of the journey talking about the sort of stunts I have to do for the film, and by the time we reach the airport, the image of Mum on the pavement is forgotten. And now, as we walk through the glass double doors, I can't wipe the smile off my face. It's just like in the films—people and bags everywhere, babies crying, flight attendants with scarves around their necks.

'Over here,' yells a voice.

We join the back of a long line where I recognize some film crew. Conner starts chatting to them, while I look around. There's an empty desk to the left of us with the sign First Class. All the other check-in desks are heaving. Only two are going to Papua New Guinea. Others are going to Mexico, Thailand, Germany.

'Kid, you look like it's your birthday,' says Conner.

'This is way better than any birthday.'

Suddenly journalists and photographers pile into the room, and there's an explosion of flashing bulbs. Girly squeals ring out. A mob of people swarms towards the First Class desk beside us.

'And Blake Saunders has entered the building,' says Conner.

I can't see Blake—he must be in the middle of the mob—when someone grabs my elbow.

'You're in the wrong line.'

Turning around, I stiffen. The man holding my elbow towers over everyone, and I recognize him straight away.

'Novak sent me to get you,' he says.

'Who are you?' says Conner.

'Finn's minder. The name's Truck.'

'But you're Novak's bodyguard. You came to my house.'

'Now I'm your minder and tutor,' he says, disgust oozing from every word.

'Conner's my mind—'

'Not any more,' says Truck grabbing my suitcase, and pulling me out of the queue.

I look to Conner who merely shrugs. 'If Novak wants you, you'd better go.'

Gripping my elbow even harder, Truck pushes me towards the swarming crowd to our left.

'Out the way!' he barks.

Taking one look at him, everyone moves. At first they stare at me with interest, then seeing I'm a nobody, they crane forward again, hoping to catch a glimpse of Blake. Before I know it, I'm at the front of the check-in with Anna and the child superstar himself.

'Good! You made it,' says Blake, smiling at me.

I glance over my shoulder to see if he's talking to someone else, when a multitude of flashes blind me.

'Don't mind them,' says Blake, putting his arm over my shoulder, so my back is to the paparazzi.

Why's he being so nice? I feel like I'm in some parallel universe.

'Here,' says Truck, thrusting a small booklet in my hands.

No way!!! It's a passport. My very own passport.

'Hand it to the lady behind the desk,' says Blake, squeezing my shoulder ever so slightly.

Reluctantly, I hand it over, but she's not even looking at me. She can't seem to take her eyes off Blake. *You're old enough to be his mother!*

CHAPTER 12

Truck ushers us through security. The paparazzi can't follow us through here, but they keep shouting, 'Blake Saunders' or 'Anna Morrow' hoping one of them will turn around. I look back and wave. Truck almost rips my shoulder out of its socket, twisting me back around again.

'You're supposed to be invisible,' he growls.

'Then why am I with them?'

'Novak's orders.'

As soon as we enter the departure lounge, Blake and Anna are mobbed again, this time by passengers.

'Sign this for my granddaughter.'

'Can I take a selfie with you?'

Blake and Anna smile graciously, and sign as many autographs as they can, while walking amazingly fast. The crowds vanish once we arrive at the departure gate, and so does Blake's smile. He drops his hand luggage at my feet.

'Take this on the plane for me,' he says.

'Take it on yourself,' says Anna in horror.

I'm about to say something similar, when I notice the AD approach us, a pained expression on his face.

'Sure,' I say, heaving the bag over my shoulder, and the AD smiles in relief.

We follow a flight attendant through a long metal tunnel until we're on board. I've seen aeroplanes in films before, but they've never looked like this. People are normally cramped together, hardly any legroom. Here, there are individual stations, with chairs that recline into beds, along with pillows and blankets. Each seat has its own TV screen that's bigger than the one in my lounge, as well as a personal fridge full of soft drinks and chocolate. I'm shown to my seat, and the flight attendant puts Blake's bag and mine into the overhead locker. Without thinking, I swipe the hat from my head.

'Your hair,' says Anna, her eyes widening.

I forgot about that!

'It makes you look like—'

'Don't say it,' I warn, and Anna grins.

She settles into the station next to mine and stretches out her arms. 'Welcome to First Class, Finn.'

'I could get used to this.'

'I wouldn't if I were you,' says Blake, from the other side of the aisle. 'Just so you know—you look nothing like me.'

'Good,' I say, but his headphones are already in his ears.

✳

The next ten hours pass in a fantastic blur. I watch the UK disappear as we rise into the sky. I play computer games for hours, joke about with Anna, and eat amazing meals—the sort I see on MasterChef. At last, the cabin crew dim the lights and everyone drifts off to sleep. Well I think they do—they no longer watch films on their private screens, and they've reclined their seats. As much as I try, sleep refuses to come. I'm just not tired. Sitting up, I press a button on my remote control. A map of the world fills the screen, and lines tracking our journey show we're over China, about halfway there. Anna told me Novak put on these planes herself. Normally you can't fly direct to Papua New Guinea.

I grab my bag and look at the script for tomorrow's filming. I can't concentrate though; my legs are beginning to ache. I never stay still for this long. Clambering out of my seat, I walk up the aisle, when a flight attendant hurries towards me.

'Can I get you something?' he whispers.

'I just want to walk. Is that okay?'

'Of course,' he replies, returning to his station, behind the curtain.

I pace up and down beside the passengers, listening to snores and heavy breathing. I was right—everyone is asleep. Should I tickle Blake's ear or do something equally annoying? I walk in between Novak and Truck, when I hear a hiss. One of them's making a strange noise. There's another hiss and my eyes dart upwards. The sound's coming from an overhead locker.

What the . . .?

Glancing about, I can't see a flight attendant. As quietly as I can, I pull open the compartment door to find a large sports bag, and by the shape of it, there's a rectangular box inside. There's another hiss and something moves against the fabric of the bag. My muscles tense. There's only one thing that can be. Who the hell brought this? Grabbing the door again, ready to slam it, my heart stops. A snake, the size of a pencil, oozes through a hole in the bag.

I freeze. The creature stares at me, its tiny tongue flickering, before darting forward as if to attack. I leap backwards, and the snake drops over the edge of the locker. It lands on the floor, curling into a spiral. What do I do now? I can't pick it up—it might be poisonous. But I can't leave it here—it might hurt itself or someone else. Novak and Truck are either side of me, still fast asleep.

'Don't move,' I whisper, running back to my seat.

I grab my pillow, yank off the cover and shove my

hand inside as if it's a glove. This will stop the venom—
not! Hurrying back, the snake is still a lump on the floor.
I take a deep breath and clasp it with two hands. Its
muscles move beneath my palms.

'What are you doing?'

My head jerks round. Blake is standing behind me,
the flight attendant behind him.

'I was just going for a walk,' I croak, keeping my back
to him, when sharp fangs stab the inside of my hand.

Somehow I swallow the scream.

CHAPTER

13

The snake wriggles even more. *Don't bite me again!* Fighting the urge to drop it, I step past Blake and the flight attendant, and find my seat. I throw the snake into my open rucksack and zip it up in record time. By the time Blake's beside me, I'm shoving the bag into the overhead locker.

'Are you wearing a pillowcase?' he asks.

'My hands were cold,' I say, falling into my chair.

Blake eyes me suspiciously but doesn't say a thing. As soon as he returns to his own station, I yank off the pillowcase, and look at my hand. Blood oozes out of two fang marks. Is poison spreading through me?

'Are you okay?'

I jump, and turn to see Anna sitting up.

'You look like you've seen a ghost.'

'I'm fine,' I mutter.

'Are you airsick?'

'I need the toilet.'

Without another word, I hurry to the small cubicle and lock the door. Falling onto the closed toilet seat, I feel cold, sweaty, dizzy. What do people do when they're bitten? Suddenly I think of a film I've seen, and I slam my lips to my wrist. Starting to suck, I will the poison to leave my body. I spit the mixture of red blood, saliva, and hopefully, venom into the small sink. I draw out more and more blood. There's a knock at the door.

'Finn, are you all right?' calls Anna.

'Yeah,' I lie.

'Do you want me to get someone?'

Who?

I lean back against the wall and look at my stinging wrist. It looks like I've given myself a giant love bite. Two pinpricks of blood appear. *Let it just be blood.* Slowly, I stand and open the door.

'You look dreadful,' says Anna. She's obviously been waiting for me.

'Thanks,' I mutter, and she grins.

She takes my arm and leads me back to my seat, while Blake watches us.

'I know you're up to something,' he says.

'Can't you just leave him alone? He's sick,' snaps Anna.

I close my eyes, trying to blot out everything, everyone. I hear passengers waking up, and Anna telling Truck that I'm ill.

'Give him another sick bag,' says Truck. 'And don't let him be sick near me. I hate the smell.'

At last I fall asleep, and when I wake up, I realize I've missed breakfast.

'Truck ate it,' says Anna apologetically. 'But I'm sure you could order something now. We're in First Class. They serve anything at any time.' Then she looks at me searchingly. 'How are you feeling?'

I sit up. 'I feel okay,' I say in surprise. *Did I do it? Did I get rid of the venom?*

'You look better. But then you couldn't have looked worse.'

Blake just stares at me, his eyes narrow.

For the rest of the journey I watch films, but there's no way I can concentrate on them. My hand stings, and every so often, I glance up at the compartment above my head. What am I going to do with my bag—with the snake—when we land? Then it hits me. My passport is in my pocket. There's nothing in my bag that I have to keep. I can borrow someone else's script.

I'm sorry, snake, but I'm going to have to 'forget' my bag.

I can't see another way.

At last we begin to descend. People are looking out the window, but all I want to do is escape the plane.

Finally the wheels hit the tarmac, and we stand in the aisles waiting to get out. The cabin crew open the plane door, and we start to move. *I'm going to get away with it!*

'Hey, muppet brain, forget something?' says Truck.

I turn as my rucksack flies through the air. Out of instinct, I catch it. The bag squirms and the hairs on the back of my neck shoot up. I'm going to have to ditch this as soon as I can.

Holding my bag way out in front, I step off the aeroplane onto a metal staircase. The heat slams into me, as we walk down metal steps straight onto the runway. A crowd of people in local dress or suits huddle around Blake, Anna, and Novak, piling flower garlands round their necks. Photographers go crazy. I stand beside Truck, away from the crowd. He's carrying Blake's rucksack, and then my heart skips a beat. He's also holding a large sports bag, the one from the overhead compartment. I know he didn't bring it on the plane. I try to take a closer look, but as far as I can tell, nothing's moving inside.

The snake in my bag decides to hiss. I glance up at Truck, but he's staring straight ahead. He swallows, and I realize he thinks the hisses are coming from his sports bag, and so I pretend to hear nothing.

At last the photographers seem satisfied, and we walk across the runway to two helicopters, hot air rippling over the tarmac.

'Don't we have to get our passports stamped?' says Anna.

74

Novak shakes her head. 'I've arranged it so we go straight to the hotel.'

'Where's everyone else?' I say, looking back at the plane. 'Where's Conner?'

'They will be allowed off when we leave,' says Novak. 'We cannot have people wandering about when the rotor blades are on. Now, who wants to fly with me?'

'I do,' says Blake.

Anna steps forward, but I grab her arm, whispering, 'I wouldn't if I were you.'

She throws me a confused look, but steps back. Novak climbs into the pilot's seat and Blake's jaw drops.

'Come on,' says Truck. 'Before she makes one of us get in there too.'

We hurry over to the second helicopter, and to my relief there's an actual pilot in the front. Climbing into the back, I drop my bag as far as I can from my feet. Luckily the rotor blades mask all hissing.

I wish I could enjoy the view but all I can think about is the snake. We soar over Port Moresby, the capital, over clusters of stone houses, shops, mazes of roads. Then the buildings spread out, the roofs become corrugated iron, interspersed with wasteland and burnt-out cars. And soon all signs of human life disappear, replaced with trees so thick you can't see anything below.

Suddenly Truck sits up. 'Listen carefully, the pair of you, and tell Blake when we get out. I should have told you earlier. Novak doesn't want any of you going anywhere without me. And don't even think about exploring the jungle. Crocodiles and cannibals live in Papua New Guinea.'

'That's not true,' says Anna. 'No one's reported cannibals living here for a long time.'

Truck snorts. 'Well if you've been eaten, you can't exactly report it, can you?'

CHAPTER 14

As soon as we arrive at the hotel, we're given a mini tour. Now I know why we came by air. The hotel is flanked by the beach on one side and thick jungle everywhere else. There are no roads leading in or out of the place. This is the sort of hotel that Mum drools at on TV. There are swimming pools that look like lagoons, immaculate gardens, and massive chandeliers hanging in five star restaurants. There's a games room, cinema, tennis courts, gym, spa, and I haven't even seen all of it yet.

Blake, Anna, Truck, and I have four rooms next to each other on the second floor of the main building. I don't know what their rooms look like, but mine is enormous. It has a four-poster bed, mini-fridge, TV, giant fan, and walk-in shower with lizard—not sure that's supposed to be there.

Truck's given us time to settle in or take a nap. This is my chance. I grab my bag, and sneak into the corridor. Not wanting to meet anyone in the escalators, I run down the two flights of stairs and out into the scorching heat.

'Good afternoon, Can I help you at all?' asks a man, wearing a pristine white uniform. He's watering a bed of the brightest coloured flowers I've ever seen.

'I'm . . . going exploring. That's all right, isn't it?'

'Of course. Enjoy.'

I hurry to the back of the hotel, where the grounds are overgrown, and the buildings more industrial. Potholes destroy the paths, and I'm sure tourists aren't supposed to be here. I reach the thick wall of trees and ferns, where the jungle begins, and strange animal calls almost deafen me. Kneeling down, I grab the zip of my bag.

'What are you doing?'

I almost leap off the ground. Scrambling to my feet, I say, 'Novak, I didn't hear you.'

'Evidently.'

There's a loud hiss, and her eyes widen. 'What's in there?'

I rub the back of my neck. There's no easy way to say this. 'I . . . I found a snake on the plane.'

Her eyes widen even more, and before I know it, I'm

telling her the whole story. She grabs my arm, turning it over.

'You were bitten?'

'Yeah—but I sucked out the poison and I feel fine.'

She shakes her head. 'The poison won't affect you yet. Your nausea was from shock. Most likely the venom is still in you.'

My mouth dries.

'Don't worry. I have an antidote. I would not bring these creatures over here without one. Fetch your bag.'

While we walk quickly back to the hotel, I keep glancing at the fang marks.

'Why did you bring them over?' I blurt. 'I didn't think that was allowed.'

'You English are so worried about rules. If you must know, the adders are my props. I want them for my film.'

'Aren't there snakes in Papua New Guinea you could use?'

'I want adders. And I do not want to work with Papuan death adders.'

'Papuan what?' I glance about.

'But tell me—were you honestly going to release my snake into the wild? It could have died. Or it could have changed the natural order in the jungle. Finn, you never release animals that are not native.'

'Sorry,' I mutter.

We travel in the elevator to the penthouse suite, and if I thought my room was nice, it's nothing compared to hers. The lounge is enormous, with chandeliers, thick squishy rugs, and a huge computer setup. There's also a massive glass tank with sleeping adders inside. A smaller, see-through container's beside it, with air holes—a travel case for snakes. That's what must have been inside the sports bag.

'I drugged them,' she explains. 'But I do not think I gave enough to the one that bit you.'

'I think you missed it out.'

'No. If he had been fully alert, there is no way you would have caught him. Adders are far too quick, and he would have bitten you many more times. Please add him to the tank.'

What?

But I can't look soft in front of her. I take a deep breath and pull the lid off the tank. To my utter relief none of the snakes move—they're obviously still drugged. I unzip my bag and hold it over the tank. I want to tip it upside down, but that means all my stuff will fall out. While wondering what to do, the snake solves my problem. The adder wriggles out on its own and drops onto the other sleeping snakes.

'Ah, it's a baby, that's why he fitted through the holes,' says Novak.

'Am I . . . going to have to do a stunt with them?'

'Not unless you want to. Should I write in a new scene?'

'No, no,' I say quickly.

I put the lid back on the tank, while Novak unclips a medical case and pulls out a needle.

'Finn, you do realize you can trust me. If you have a problem like an escaped snake, you can tell me. You do not have to hide anything,' she says. 'Hold out your arm.'

I can't watch. Turning away, I feel a sharp stab, when someone starts banging on the door to her suite.

'Novak, are you there?' It's Alistair. 'Novak, it's on Gamboi Island.'

'I'm coming,' shouts Novak, sharply. She drops the needle back into the medical case and shoves it under a cushion on the sofa. 'Alistair does not need to hear about this,' she whispers, before opening the door.

Alistair marches inside. 'I've spoken to some locals and—' He stops as soon as he sees me. 'What are you doing here?'

'I sent for him,' says Novak. 'We've been going over some of his stunts. But I was telling him that we won't start work until the day after tomorrow, as everyone will be suffering from jet lag.'

She was?

'Finn, you should go back to your room and catch some sleep.' She glances at my wrist. 'You have nothing to worry about. Your stunts will be fine.'

I know she's not taking about my stunts, and I smile in relief. With Alistair's eyes boring into the back of my skull, I leave the room.

'He shouldn't be here,' says Alistair, his voice drifting

through the door. 'He's too young for this. He's not capable.'

My jaw clenches. I am getting so fed up with him. I'll show Alistair just how capable I am.

CHAPTER

15

I spend the next two days getting over jet lag, getting used to the heat, and exploring the hotel with Anna. Our favourite game is hiding from Truck. We don't see Blake, since he stays in his room, only appearing at mealtimes.

'What do you think he does in there?' says Anna.

'Perfects his smouldering smile in the mirror,' I say, pouting and making my eyes steely.

'You look like a duck.'

'That's the look I was going for.'

'I think he's practising his Oscar speech.' She clears her throat. 'I wouldn't be here today without the help of—'

'Daddy,' we both say at the same time and burst into hysterics.

It's amazing. I've only known her a few days but I feel as though we've been mates for years. Sam would fancy her so much. She's not my type though.

'I reckon he's still getting over his journey with Novak. I heard he was really sick,' says Anna.

'There's no way you would ever get me in a—'

'Hey you two, you're wanted on set,' calls Truck.

Whoa! I want to record him saying that. Finally, someone's calling me to be on set!

Truck hands me a beige bundle before leaving me in hair, make-up, and wardrobe. For the first time since it was cut, I'm glad of my new hairstyle—no more wigs and pins jabbing into my head. After I'm transformed into Rio, Truck takes me to the beach. Golden sand, crystal blue waters. I'm in paradise. I join Conner, who's watching Blake act out a scene.

'He's good,' whispers Conner.

'I know,' I mutter. *I wish he wasn't.*

'Have you got your jerk vest? I gave it to Truck.'

'I've got it, but I don't need it. I can climb a tree without wires.'

'You're climbing a palm, not an oak. There are no branches low down. Anyway, Alistair insisted.'

'He only insisted because he thinks I'm not good enough.'

'That's not true,' says Conner, shaking his head. 'He

feels responsible. He's concerned for your well-being.' He looks past me, then adds, 'You must be up. Novak's beckoning us.'

'I don't need a jerk vest,' I say, as soon as we reach her. 'There's no need for a crane.'

Novak's eyes light up. 'Perfect, I was hoping you'd say that.'

Conner looks like he wants to kill me, but keeps his mouth shut.

I head to the spot where Blake was standing, and replicate his pose. This is where I become Rio. Then I glance at the film crew, searching for Alistair. How can I prove myself to him when he isn't even here?

'We will rehearse once before we start filming,' says Novak.

I already have! This morning, I snuck into the gardens, and watched some of the staff climbing the trees for coconuts. When they left, I practised myself. I'm glad I did. It's harder than they made it look.

'Action!'

I grab the trunk of the palm and almost hug it. Then planting my feet so they curl around the rough bark, I begin to climb. Like a monkey, higher and higher, with no need for wires. At the top, I lean forward and punch a coconut. It wobbles a little, but that's it. Why didn't I practise this bit? I punch again. It stays where it is.

'Cut!'

Heat flushes through me, as I climb back down. I had

one job. I peer out of the corner of my eyes at Novak. Her lips are pressed tight, and Blake is standing next to her, grinning smugly. *Argh!*

'We need more urgency, and a knife to cut down the coconuts,' says Novak.

'What about a machete? That's what the locals use,' says the AD.

'Hold up,' says Conner, stepping forward, his hand out flat. 'You want a fourteen-year-old boy to climb that tree without wires while carrying a razor-sharp machete?'

'Yes. Do you have a problem with that?' says Novak.

'Do you?' says Conner, looking directly at me.

'I'll be fine,' I say.

Conner raises his eyebrows and shakes his head, but he can't disagree with Novak.

'What about a blunt machete?' says the AD.

'A blunt machete will not cut down the coconuts,' snaps Novak. 'We need it to be sharp.'

Less than a minute later, a man appears carrying a belt with a leather sheath attached, the handle of a knife peeking out. I move to take it, when he pulls the belt out of my grasp.

'He's a child. He can't touch this,' says the man, with a strong local accent.

'He is a very capable child, and I will pay you well,' says Novak.

The man tilts his head, seemingly wrestling with his conscience. At last he hands me the belt, and I fasten it around my middle, pulling it to its tightest notch. It's still slightly baggy and the sheath dangles down.

'We will film this take,' says Novak.

The cameramen get ready, while I wait at the base of the tree.

'You sure you're okay with this?' says Conner.

I nod.

'Where the hell is Alistair? He would put a stop to it,' he mutters, walking out of the shot.

'Scene 74. Cameras ready? Lighting ready?' says the AD. He snaps the clapperboard. 'Take one! Action!'

I grab onto the trunk and climb, the machete banging into my thigh. I'm glad it's sheathed. Novak said 'urgency' so I imagine I'm being chased. I climb faster, but my feet slip, and I jump back down to the ground.

'Cut.'

They have to reset the cameras and I look down, not wanting to catch anyone's eye.

'Scene 74. Cameras ready? Lighting ready? Take two. Action.'

I clasp the trunk. *The baddies are behind me.* I have to move quickly, but not rush so much that I make mistakes. My feet curl around the base and I pull myself up—higher and higher. Ignoring the bang of the machete, I reach the top, and yank the blade out of its sheath. With the metal glinting in the sunlight, I lean forward and swipe at the stalk of the coconut. It cuts some strands but not enough. I hack again and the coconut hurtles to the ground. Using one hand I cling to the top, while I use the other to slide the machete into the sheath . . . except it won't go in. I try again, but I need two hands.

There's no way I can let Novak down again.

Keeping one arm wrapped around the trunk, I hold the machete in the air. Using my feet and knees, I start to descend, but my feet slip. I slide down the trunk, the bark ripping through my palm and knees, the pain shooting through me. I land, still holding the machete. Copying the way Blake runs, I hurtle into the jungle.

'Cut!'

I did it!

Walking back to the palm tree, there's silence. No cheering. The cameramen, the AD, Conner . . . and Alistair (I don't know when he arrived) stare at me in horror. Did I do something wrong?

Then Novak says, 'Absolutely brilliant.' She pops out from behind a camera. 'I've just watched your take and you were amazing. A true superstar.'

'A true nutter,' someone mutters.

'We need to do two more takes just like that,' says Novak.

Two? My hands and knees are killing me.

Alistair steps forward. 'If it was so amazing, couldn't we just leave it at that?'

'You of all people should know I do a minimum of three takes whenever I can,' says Novak.

'In that case, he needs bandaging up. He needs gloves

and kneepads. And a jerk vest,' says Alistair.

'He does not. Do you, Finn?' says Novak.

'I can do it without.'

'This is a lawsuit waiting to happen,' says Alistair.

'Only if someone finds out,' says Novak. 'Finn, you need to clean up. We can't have you starting out with blood. While you do that, we will redo the shoot with Blake. He needs to be wearing the machete belt.'

Blake wanders over to us, taking the belt from me. 'Someone needs to clean the tree,' he says casually. 'There's blood all down it.'

CHAPTER
16

I toss and turn in bed. My hands and knees are raw.
The buzz of the air-conditioning is driving me mad,
and it's not even working that well. I'm still hot and
sweaty. I give up. Novak told us to have an early night,
but I can't stay here. I change into swimming shorts
and grab the robe the hotel has provided. Easing open
my bedroom door, I tiptoe down the dimly-lit hallway
towards the stairs. I hear a creak and freeze.

Please not Truck.

Turning around, I see Anna in a matching robe.

'Couldn't you sleep either?' she whispers.

I shake my head.

'Walk?' she mouths.

'Swim.'

Her face breaks into a giant grin. 'Wait one sec,' she mouths, before darting into her room.

Minutes later, she's back, and we tiptoe down the two flights of stairs. We dart through the lobby—luckily the reception desk is empty—and head outside. The place is deserted of people, but the noise from crickets, frogs, and whatever else is out there, is deafening. The smell of flowers seems even stronger at night.

We hurry down paths lit by neon lanterns, until we reach the pool. It's beautiful—a stone lagoon rather than a swimming pool. There are two bridges, plus a waterfall that's competing for noise with the insects. Chucking my robe onto a nearby sunlounger, I hook my toes over the edge. Can I dive-bomb or will that make too much noise? Then I feel two hands and I plummet into water. My cuts sting for a split second, and I swallow back a yelp. Anna pushed me in!

She slides in beside me, laughing quietly.

'Noise,' I mouth.

'It was only a splash,' she whispers. 'No one would have heard it over the waterfall.'

I'm beginning to think I should have left her at the hotel.

'Race you to the bridge,' she says, already swimming for it.

No way am I going to let her win. I grab her foot, yank her back, and power past. Tapping the underside of the bridge, I whisper, 'Loser,' as she reaches me.

'*Urgh*, your hands,' she says, her nose wrinkling. 'Are they from your stunt earlier? Everyone was talking about it.'

Peering at the scabs and grazes, I say, 'They're all right now.'

Anna shakes her head, 'I'm trying to work out if you're brave or stupid. Blake thinks you're the second.'

I roll my eyes. 'He should be pleased I'm here. I can't believe how little he does. He's such a wuss, so scared of getting hurt.'

'I think it's part of his contract. They can't afford to have him injured.' She pauses. 'I'm not allowed to do much either. I've—'

We hear voices, and her mouth clamps shut. I grab her hand and pull her further under the bridge. We can't be caught.

The voices get louder:

'There's no way we could have got any closer.' *That's Alistair!*

'She's going to need someone who speaks the language or they're dead,' says a voice I don't recognize.

'I'll let Novak know,' says Alistair. 'But you know what she's like. She'll make them do it anyway.'

Anna and I stare at each other. *What are they talking about?*

Silently, we peer out from under the bridge. Five men hobble past the pool towards the lobby. One of them towers over everyone else, limping badly.

'Is that Truck?' whispers Anna.

'You're right!'

'What's he got in his bag?'

I look at the rucksack dangling from his hand; an electric blue light shines out through the canvas, brighter than most floodlights.

'Must be a torch,' I say.

The men disappear down a path, and after a minute or two, Anna and I climb out. Shivering, I head for our robes. Thank God the men didn't notice them even though they walked straight past. Then I stop. For the ground is covered in blood. *What on earth happened to them?*

∗

'I'll pour this over you.'

My eyes flash open to see a glass of water tilted above my head.

'Oh! You've woken up,' groans Truck, straightening up the glass.

'You sound disappointed.'

'I am.'

He moves backwards and I sit bolt upright, remembering last night. I look at his legs.

'How are you feeling?' I ask.

He throws me a funny look. 'Fine. Why?'

'Aren't you hot, wearing long trousers?'

93

'I didn't bring enough shorts. I need to go to the launderette.' Then his curious expression turns to a wicked smile. 'Unlike some, my mummy didn't check how many underpants I packed.'

I can't believe Conner told them what Mum said. I'm going to kill him!

Then I lie back down, my head spinning. Did I dream last night? Did I even go swimming?

'What are you doing?' demands Truck. 'You're wanted on set in about an hour. You need to wash, have breakfast, speak to Conner.'

He tilts the glass above my head again, and I roll out of bed the other side, landing on something damp. Wet swimming shorts! I need to see Anna.

'If you get out, I can get dressed,' I say, jumping to my feet.

Truck nods, before shuffling awkwardly across the room.

'Are you limping?' I say.

'Yeah—I slept funny. Gave myself a dead leg.'

I know you're lying!

He disappears into the hallway and I get ready as fast as humanly possible. Five minutes later, I'm in the restaurant, walking past the long table covered with pastries, pancakes, bacon—you name it. Where is Anna?

I pile waffles and pancakes onto my plate, and drown them in maple syrup, before joining Truck. He's tucking into a bowl of cereal and fruit.

94

'That's not exactly healthy,' he says, eying my plate.

'At least mine doesn't look as though it was found at the bottom of a rabbit hutch.'

Shovelling in a forkful, I notice two men from last night further down the table; one has a massive fresh scratch across his face.

'What happened to him?' I say.

'I don't know. Probably hurt himself on set,' says Truck. 'Will you stop staring? Didn't your mother tell you it was rude?'

I tear my eyes away from the scar and scan the room. 'Where are Anna and Blake?'

'They were up at 4. Novak decided to do an early shoot.'

4? Anna must be exhausted.

Suddenly I spot Alistair and Conner heading our way, their faces grimmer than I've ever seen before. My stomach drops. Do they know I was in the pool? Was Conner there last night?

Alistair jabs his finger at me. 'This is your fault. Novak now thinks—'

'Hey, wait a minute,' says Conner. 'You can't blame Finn. He *is* a stunt actor. He had nothing to do with Anna. And Anna begged Novak to let her do it—said she was capable.'

'What are you talking about?' I say.

Alistair grimaces even more.

'Has something happened to Anna?' I ask.

CHAPTER 17

'What is it? What's happened to her?' I ask.

Alistair says, 'Novak made Anna—'

'Let Anna,' corrects Conner.

'Made, let—who cares?' says Alistair. 'Anna did her own stunt this morning. She's never had any training but since you . . .'

Their words fade into the distance as I relive my conversation with Anna from last night. 'Such a wuss. Doesn't dare get hurt.'

I was talking about Blake not her.

'And now they're calling the hospital, her parents,' says Alistair.

His words jerk me to the present. 'She's hurt?'

'Yeah,' says Conner gently.

'Yes!' snaps Alistair.

'Where is she?' I say, leaping to my feet.

Conner's eyes fill with pity, 'She can't see anyone. Novak is keeping her in—'

'Where is she?' I yell.

'She's in the doctor's room, behind the—'

I don't wait to hear Conner's directions. Anna and I found it when we explored the hotel. I tear out of the restaurant, dodging film crew, and run down numerous hallways. The AD blocks the doctor's door.

'She's not allowed visitors,' he says.

'But I'm her friend.'

'We're all her friends.'

'Is Blake in with her?'

'I had to let him through.'

'Then you have to let me in too.'

'Sorry Kid.' He shakes his head.

Suddenly a member of the hotel staff in a smart suit appears at the end of the corridor. 'Excuse me,' she calls. 'Are you the AD? There's a phone call for you from London.'

The AD nods, then turns and points at me. 'Don't go in. That's a direct order.'

He hurries down the corridor, following the member of staff, and I slip into the room. My heart stops. Anna is lying on a bed, eyes closed, her left leg elevated in some kind of splint. Blake is sitting in a chair beside her, his face pale and drawn.

'Anna,' I whisper.

'She's unconscious,' says Blake.

My stomach lurches. 'What happened?'

'She wanted to jump in herself. From the cliff, without wires.' He gulps, like he's swallowing sick. 'I should have stopped her, but I was too busy practising my lines. I wasn't paying attention.' He looks up at me, his eyes wet. 'I didn't think we were going to do that part of the scene. I thought we were going to have our conversation, before you and her stunt double turned up.'

His words drip like poison through my veins. I made her do this.

'It's my fault,' says Blake.

'It's really not,' I say. Tears sting my eyes and I blink hard, willing them to go away.

The door opens and I expect the AD, but a doctor enters, her lips pursing at the sight of us.

'What are you doing in here?' she demands.

'We wanted to see our friend,' says Blake.

'No one is allowed. You might be some sort of superstar, but she is my patient and she needs rest. So get out. The pair of you.'

She holds the door open and we traipse out of the room. In silence, we head to our own floor, where Truck is waiting.

'Novak says we won't be filming today. So you two have the day off.'

Without saying anything, we disappear into our own rooms.

I spend the rest of the day hiding, even refusing to come out at mealtimes. The thought of food makes me sick. That night, I crawl into bed, fully dressed. I wish I could get that conversation from the pool out of my head. No, that's not true. I wish I could talk to her.

There's a loud bang on my door.

'Go away, Truck,' I shout.

'She's awake!'

I jump out of bed, and whisk open the door. 'How is she?'

'She's all right. I was just speaking to her,' says Truck. 'She's going back to the US in a few hours.'

'The US? Doesn't she have to go to hospital?'

'Her mum wants to get her back home—have it sorted out there.'

I brush my hands through my hair. 'Can I see her? I really need to before she goes.'

'That's why I'm here. She wants to talk to you.'

Barefoot, I race down the corridors. Truck keeps up, and to my surprise doesn't make me slow down. I reach the doctor's door, and lift my arm to knock. But now I'm here, I'm terrified. *What can I say to her?*

Truck leans over me and knocks on the door much more daintily than he did on mine. 'We haven't got all night.'

'Come in,' croaks Anna.

Taking a deep breath, I walk inside.

'I'll be out here,' says Truck.

Anna is sitting upright, her leg in a different splint this time.

'You look better,' I say.

'I don't feel it, but I'm a brave little actress,' she says with a strained laugh.

I try to smile. 'What happened exactly?'

'I'm not allowed to say.'

I raise my eyebrows.

'She is under contract, just like you,' says Novak.

My heart jumps into my throat and I spin round. Novak's sitting in a chair at the back of the room.

'I persuaded Novak to let me do my own stunt, but I had to sign a form first,' says Anna.

'A confidentiality agreement,' adds Novak.

Turning to face my friend again, I blurt, 'I'm sorry.' I can feel Novak's eyes burning into me, but if I don't say it now—when can I?

'Whatever for?' says Anna.

'When we talked about stunts, I didn't mean for you to try them. I didn't mean you were a wuss.'

'You called Anna a wuss?' says Novak.

'No. I called—'

'Finn,' says Anna sharply. 'It was nothing to do with you. It was my choice.' She looks at me hard, and I get the feeling that she's trying to tell me something. 'Can I have a hug goodbye?' she asks.

A hug? I'm not used to hugging girls. 'Yeah . . . I guess.'

I lean over the bed and she wraps her arms around me. I try not to tense but fail miserably. As I pull away, she grabs my hands, and I realize she's stuffing a piece of paper into my right palm. Squeezing my hands, she says, 'I'm going to miss you.'

'I'm going to miss you too.'

'Good luck with the rest of the film.'

Novak clasps her hands together. 'You two have such great chemistry. Perhaps you should work together as the leading stars in my next film.'

I grin at Anna and she smiles back. But the smile doesn't reach her eyes.

'You'd better go. I need to get ready,' she says.

Truck escorts me back to my room. I head straight to the bathroom, which has the only door Truck can't unlock. Then I unravel the crumpled piece of paper.

CHAPTER 18

I read and reread the words.

Don't trust Novak—she's not what she seems!

The next morning at breakfast, Anna and the note are all I can think about. What does she mean? What happened between the pair of them?

'We need a new actress,' says Blake, sliding into the seat opposite me,

I put down my spoon. 'Don't you think it's a bit soon to be worried about that? Anna's only just left. She was injured.'

He shrugs. 'I'm sorry Anna was hurt, but the film must go on. There are budgets and—'

'Can you hear yourself? I thought you felt responsible.

Last night, you—'

'I'm actually hoping Novak chooses someone a bit more professional this time. Someone who doesn't whisper and giggle with you.'

I grip onto the sides of the table. 'You do realize there's more to life than filming?'

Blake looks at me like I've just shot his dad. Then he leans back and folds his arms. 'Get me a bowl of fruit. No melon. I hate melon.'

'Get it yourself,' I say, channelling Anna. She might not be here in body but—

Then I hear the clearing of a throat. You have got to be joking! The AD is sitting at the table beside us. I scrape back my chair and stomp over to the breakfast buffet.

*

Over the next couple of days, Blake continues ordering me about, always when the AD is present so I can't refuse. We carry on filming the scenes where Anna isn't needed. I fall down stairs, climb more palm trees, scoot down drainpipes. Blake is doing even fewer action shots now. If Novak didn't hate CGI so much, they could just superimpose his head on my body for the entire film.

After a particularly long shoot, working with the AD, Blake and I cut through the lobby. Novak is sitting at a coffee table with a really fit girl about our age. She has light brown skin, tight brown curly hair, amazing cheekbones. I straighten my back and walk a little taller.

'Ah boys,' says Novak, beckoning us over. 'Let me introduce you to—'

'You're Blake Saunders,' gushes the girl in a local accent. She leaps to her feet. 'I've seen all your films.'

Oh great!

Novak's mobile rings and she smiles apologetically, before moving away to take the call in private.

Blake gives the girl one of his smouldering smiles. 'It's always nice to meet a fan. Would you like an autograph?'

The girl gasps. I roll my eyes.

'Have you got paper and pen?' says Blake.

'I didn't think to bring any,' she says, looking anxious.

'Finn, go get the girl some paper and a pen.'

The girl looks at me for the first time as if she's surprised I'm even here. The AD is nowhere to be seen and so I fold my arms, opening my mouth to tell him to 'stuff it' when the girl smiles at me and says, 'Would you?'

Next thing I know, I'm on the other side of the lobby, next to a desk and pressing the bell for a receptionist to come. Novak is pacing the carpet, looking agitated. 'Are you sure—five days? That's quicker than I thought. No, no, they'll be ready. I'll make sure of it.'

'Can I help you?' says the receptionist, coming to the desk.

Seconds later, I return with the pen and paper. Blake is quoting some of his famous lines and I think the girl might actually pass out.

Even though I shouldn't, I say, 'Blake, tell her about your stunts.'

'Oh yes, I heard you do them all yourself. Is that true?' says the girl.

Blake winks at her. 'I'm not allowed to say.'

The girl grins, as if they are sharing this special secret. 'I knew it. I knew you did.'

I want to punch something. I hate my contract.

'Ah good, you are all getting to know each other,' says Novak, reappearing. She puts her hand on the girl's shoulder. 'My latest star.'

'Excuse me?' says Blake.

'This is Mawi. She'll be playing Anna's role.'

Whoa!

Mawi grins, clutching her piece of paper.

Blake's face tightens. 'Mawi,' he says slowly. 'Have you ever acted before? Have you ever been in anything?'

'An advert for my father's car company,' she says.

Blake blinks many times. 'An advert? Was it shown internationally?'

'No,' she says with a laugh. 'Only in Papua New Guinea, but people really like it, and Dad's sold two more cars already.'

'Two whole cars. Wow—you must be an amazing actor,' says Blake.

Mawi gulps, and starts fiddling with her hair.

Novak's eyes narrow. 'Blake can I have a word? Finn, you come too. Mawi, would you excuse us please? We will be right back.'

Novak leads us to the other side of the lobby. 'What do you think you're doing?' she hisses to Blake.

'You expect me to work with an amateur?'

'She is not an amateur. She has been in an advert,' says Novak.

Blake rolls his eyes.

Novak leans forward. 'You think I would choose just anyone for my film? Mawi's audition was perfect. She is a natural.'

'I bet she only got the advert job because of her father,' sneers Blake.

'Well, you and her have a lot in common then, don't you?' says Novak.

If Anna were here, she'd tell me to close my mouth. Did Novak honestly just say that?

Blake's cheeks redden and he glances at me, before returning his glare to Novak. 'My dad will be hearing about this.'

'I'll tell him myself,' says Novak. 'Your father made it perfectly clear that you are supposed to be treated like any other actor. And actors have to stay in line with their director.'

Blake knows when he's beaten. 'She'd better be good.'

'She will be,' says Novak. 'If not, then I will replace her. Nothing and I mean nothing will ruin my film.'

CHAPTER 19

'**B**lake doesn't seem happy I'm in this film,' says Mawi, fiddling with a curl.

'He'll live.'

Her eyes dart nervously to the door Blake disappeared through. He's due back any moment. He and Novak went to find a script for her since she was only given a section for her audition. Although, by the way Novak dragged Blake out of the room, I'm guessing he's in trouble—most likely for questioning the Director in front of us.

'I had to audition. I beat six other girls,' says Mawi.

Oh God! 'I wouldn't tell Blake that.'

'Why not?'

'He beat 8,000 for his role.' Although perhaps he

didn't, perhaps it was all his dad . . .

'Oh,' she says awkwardly.

Desperately trying to think of something to say, I ask, 'Have you heard of the Ropen?'

She nods. 'I think most Papuans have. My great-uncle used to talk about it all the time. He believed anyone who came in contact with the Ropen would get haunted by the spirit world. Mythological beasts would find you, feed off your energy.'

'Nice!' I say. 'What about you? Do you think it's real?'

'No,' she says, pulling a face as if I'm a muppet for even asking. 'Out of my family, only my great-uncle believed in it, and he was completely mad.' She curls another strand of hair around her finger. 'Are you an actor too?'

'Yeah.'

'Are you the villain or something because I've not seen you before?'

'I'm a stunt double.'

'Really?' she says, looking at me with more interest.

Then she smiles and little dimples form in her cheeks. I can't take my eyes off them.

'No one's supposed to know this but you're going to find out soon enough. I'm Blake's stunt double.'

'Blake's? I thought he did his own stunts.'

I shake my head. 'It's me.'

'Wow! That's amazing.'

'It's okay,' I say casually. Did she just call me amazing?

'I do gymnastics and I mountain climb,' she says, her

eyes beginning to sparkle. 'Do you think I'll be able to do my own stunts?'

'I doubt it. Ever since Anna got injured, I can't imagine Novak letting you do anything.'

'Is Anna the girl I replaced?'

I want to curl up and die. Here I am thinking about dimples, and Anna is on her way home, badly hurt.

'Blake will be here soon,' I say abruptly.

Mawi throws me a funny look, but doesn't say anything.

*

I was wrong!

Three hours later, we discover Mawi *is* doing her own stunts. At least she's harnessed—I'm not. We're standing beside a twelve-metre climbing wall Novak set up. I'm in full Rio gear. Hair, make-up, wardrobe.

'Finn, show her how it's done,' says Novak.

'Why hasn't she got a stunt double?' I ask.

Novak sighs. 'Because Anna's stunt double doesn't look anything like Mawi. They don't have the same build, skin colour, or height. So we thought she could do the easy stunts herself, while we try to find a new one.'

I glance at Alistair. He doesn't look happy.

Mawi doesn't look bothered though. She's bouncing on the balls of her feet. 'Where's Blake?' she whispers.

'He's never around unless he's in a scene. He stays in his room.'

'Oh!'

'We will rehearse a couple of times, before involving the camera crew,' says Novak. 'Finn, show her how it's done.'

I grab the nearest handhold and pull up easily. My feet and fingers find the ledges and I race to the top. Looking to the ground, Novak is clapping, but Alistair beckons me down.

'You're supposed to show her how to do it. Not show off,' he says, as I land on the grass.

'I wasn't showing off,' I say, my cheeks feeling hot.

'Yeah—course you weren't.'

My jaw clenches and I turn away from him. 'You said you can climb?' I say to Mawi.

She nods. Then tilts her head. 'Why aren't you harnessed?'

'Novak prefers not to use CGI. She doesn't like taking wires away in the edit.'

Fingers grip my shoulder from behind. 'Stop talking,' hisses Alistair in my ear.

What's his problem? Twisting out of his grip, I show Mawi where I put my hands and feet. I climb slowly so she can literally follow my footsteps, and soon we're both at the top.

'You really didn't need to show me what to do,' says Mawi with a laugh. 'This isn't exactly high. I mountain climb, remember?'

We perch on the top, looking over the hotel. It's

amazing how much we can see from here—the pools, the spa, the—

Is that Truck? I thought he was supposed to be with Blake. He's talking to someone behind a building . . . except he's not just talking, he's got his hands around the man's neck. Suddenly Truck releases him and punches the man in the face. The man collapses and rolls across the ground. My mouth dries. Should I do something? I glance at Mawi, but she's staring in the opposite direction. Then my heart stops. For Truck turns his head and looks straight at me. I almost give myself whiplash, twisting away so quickly.

'We should go back,' I say, throwing myself down the wall.

I reach the grass before she's halfway.

'You were supposed to show her the way down,' says Alistair.

Trying to push the image of Truck from my mind, I say. 'I doubt she needs my help.'

And as I look back up. Mawi glides down the wall far more gracefully than me.

Novak claps her hands. 'So impressive, both of you. Now go up again, as if you're chasing the Ropen. I need urgency.'

But Truck!

'Today, not tomorrow,' snaps Novak.

'Ready?' I say to Mawi, but she's staring over my shoulder.

'Blake's coming,' she whispers. Then in a louder voice she says, 'Novak, is there any way I can do this without a harness? I'm used to climbing.'

'No,' says Alistair, sharply, but Novak is already clapping her hands again.

'Of course you can, my girl,' she says. 'How wonderful. We have another Finn.'

Alistair glowers at me and I realize why he wanted me to stop talking earlier. I gave Mawi the idea.

Shaking his head, Alistair unclips her harness. Then he leans in to me. 'Go slowly.'

I don't need to be told. I can't let anything happen to her.

'I want urgency,' says Novak. 'And go.'

I climb carefully, when Mawi storms past, like a pro. She reaches the top before me and I hear Blake laughing. Scrambling to reach her, I try to keep my eyes away from the spa, but I can't help it—they're drawn towards it.

Truck's gone!

'Told you I can climb,' says Mawi, as soon as I'm sitting beside her.

'You're good,' I say, scanning the grounds to see if I can spot him somewhere. 'But maybe you should be a bit more caref—'

'Race you to the bottom,' she shouts, and off she goes.

Suddenly I don't care about looking for Truck. I'm not losing in front of the others. Instead of climbing, I almost jump from ledge to ledge, springing off the rocks.

I land seconds before Mawi.

'That was spectacular,' says Novak.

'What do you think, Blake?' says Mawi.

'You should have looked up more, as if there was a Ropen in the air in front of you,' he says.

Mawi's face drops. 'Oh. Yeah, of course.'

All at once I feel eyes boring into my back, and I turn to see Truck walking towards us. My pulse races, but now is the moment of truth.

'What do you think Truck? Were we fast enough?' I say, trying to sound casual, as if I haven't seen him punch a guy.

Truck lets out a sigh, and his whole body relaxes. 'I thought you were both great,' he says.

I don't believe it. He was just as nervous as me.

CHAPTER

20

The next week flies by. Mawi and I perform simple stunts together—climbing over cliffs, swinging on ropes—and I watch her act out scenes with Blake. She's always trying to get him to rehearse more, but as soon as Novak releases him, he returns to his room. I still miss Anna. I wish I could talk to her about Truck, and her note.

'I need you to catch a pig,' says Conner one afternoon, thrusting a script in my hands.

'Rio catches a pig?'

'Yeah, he's got to eat.'

'Can't he go to a restaurant?'

'In the deepest, darkest jungle in Papua New Guinea?

115

I'm guessing not.'

I scan the directions and rub the back of my neck. *It looks so complicated.* 'Why do I have to do this and not Blake? It's not exactly stunt work.'

'It's not like you to complain,' says Conner. 'But if you must know, Blake's not allowed to work with animals. It's in his—'

'Contract?' I finish.

Conner grins. 'I think he's driving Novak up the wall, but don't let anyone else hear me say that.'

'Hear you say what?' says Mawi, walking towards us.

'Nothing. You're catching a pig today,' says Conner.

'I know. We're using a snare net and toggle release.'

Conner and I look at each other, then back at Mawi.

'You sound like you know what you're talking about,' I say.

'I go hunting with Granddad every so often. Don't look so horrified. We always eat what we catch. Where do you think your meat comes from?'

'Plastic wrappers in the supermarket,' I say, and she laughs.

'Enough joking about,' says Novak, seeming to materialize out of thin air. 'We are going to film this scene soon, and for once I am hoping it will need only one take. I don't want the pig wary of the trap.'

'It's not going to hurt him, is it?' I say.

'If it does, it will be our little secret,' says Novak.

Half an hour later, the cameras are rolling. Below a

young palm tree, Mawi and I unravel a net with ropes dangling from it. She drops some food pellets into the centre. Then I pull the top of the tree so it's bending over. Mawi wraps a strong wire around the top, fastening one end to the ropes of the net, the other to a piece of whittled wood interlocking into a log staked in the ground. I can tell she's done this before.

We hurry behind the hedge, as a runner releases a pig from a cage just out of camera shot. The pig snuffles onto the net. The wire tightens, pulling the top log off the stake in the ground. The four corners of the net swoop up, swinging the pig in the air.

'Yes!' I shout, punching the sky.

'Cut!' shouts Novak, storming over. 'What were you thinking? Yes—is not in the script.'

'I'm sorry. I was just so surprised it worked.'

Novak rolls her eyes. 'You are lucky because we need to film it again anyway. Mawi, you look too efficient. You make Rio look worthless. I want you to stand back and let him do more.'

'I thought you were really good,' I whisper to Mawi.

'Everyone thought she was really good,' says Novak. 'It was you who looked ridiculous.'

We film the scene fourteen more times and use five different pigs before Novak gets her shot. This has got to be my worst day. By Novak's reactions, the pigs outshine me.

I eat dinner early, so I can be by myself, but just as I

finish, Mawi and Blake walk into the restaurant. They're both carrying a gift box, one green, one purple.

'Finn,' squeals Mawi. 'You're not going to believe what Novak gave us. She said they're perfect for her two stars.'

'"Superstars" is the exact word she used,' says Blake, with a smug grin.

They hold out their boxes, and my heart plummets.

CHAPTER 21

In the purple box, is a miniature Mawi doll—capturing her dark skin, tight curly hair, and dimples. And in the green, is a perfect Rio with black hair, blue eyes, and swooning smile. Not the arrogant leer I'm used to. A pair of sunglasses dangles from his hands.

'They're going to be sold all over the world,' says Mawi.

Papuan death adders squirm inside me. Looking up at Blake, I say, 'Aww—you have a doll.'

'It's not a doll. It's an action figure,' he says.

'Oh, it's definitely a doll. A Ken doll, all wrapped up in tissue paper. Just like you. Perhaps I should start calling you Ken.'

'You know I'm not allowed to do my own stunts,' says Blake. 'Unlike some, I'm irreplaceable. It matters if I get hurt.'

'You choose not to do your own stunts,' I say, getting to my feet. 'I guess I'll leave you two to play with your Barbie dolls. After my dinner and day of—you know—action hero stuff, I need to lie down.'

'Action hero stuff? Like trapping a pig? Exactly how many takes did you do?' says Blake.

'Well considering you couldn't even do one because you might mess up your Ken hair or break a nail, I don't think you should mock.'

'What's your problem?' says Mawi.

'He's just jealous.'

'Nothing could make me jealous of you, Blake,' I say, walking out of the restaurant.

I head back to my room, trying to get rid of Mawi's hurt expression. She'd been so happy and I killed it for her. But why does everything have to happen for Blake?

I want to throw myself on my bed, but there's a green box lying upside down on it.

This is all I need.

Novak's given me a Rio doll. Perhaps I could stick pins in it or use it as target practice. I turn the box over, ready to fling it across the room, when . . . It's not Blake—it's me. A mini-me, with blond hair like mine was before it was dyed, and my look of concentration. It's wearing a jerk vest and protective pads. I almost burst out laughing.

It's definitely an action figure. Not a Ken doll. Even the lettering on the box says, 'Stunt Double.'

I have my own merchandise.

Then I see the note:

Finn, this is for you. Unfortunately it will not be sold in the shops, as you are my greatest secret.

Novak

I hug the box to my chest, then quickly drop my hands. I'd die if anyone saw me do that! Tucking the box under my arm, I hurry out of my room and run upstairs straight for the penthouse suite. I'm about to knock on the door when I hear Novak shout from inside the room:

'This is what you signed up for!'

'Then I quit.'

The door bursts opens and a member of the camera crew flies out. He takes one look at me and says, 'If you know what's good for you, you'll quit too.'

He shuffles past and I stare at the blood seeping through his bandaged arm.

'Are you hurt?' I call.

'Hey—I'm alive. That's more than I can say for the others.'

'What?'

'Ah Finn,' says Novak, 'do come in. I've been expecting you.'

'Is he all right?' I ask, watching him limp around the corridor.

'He is fine. He hurt himself while rigging up a camera

and is now planning on suing me. Such is the life of a director.' She smiles at me. 'Did you find something on your bed?'

I nod, trying to forget about the cameraman. 'I wanted to say thank you.'

'My absolute pleasure. You work just as hard, if not harder than Blake and Mawi. I know you had a tough day today, but you made it work in the end. I had two action figures made of you.'

'Two?'

'One for your mama. I sent it to her a couple of days ago.'

'You did? You know she'll be putting it on the window-sill of our house or worse—taping it to the lamppost.'

Novak laughs. 'I made her promise to keep it inside. I said she could put it on the mantelpiece just as long as she hides it when she has guests.'

'She agreed to that?'

Panic flashes across Novak's face. 'I hope so. She can't let others know about you. Maybe I will ring her again now. Off you go.'

Returning to the second floor, I run into Blake and Mawi. Hiding my smile, I hold the box, making sure the action figure's facing out.

Blake's jaw drops. 'Why have you got one? Novak can't sell it. Everyone's got to think I do the stunts.'

'She's not selling it. But she thought I deserved one for all my hard work.'

'So you have a Barbie doll too?' says Mawi, her lips twitching.

'Oh mine is definitely an action figure,' I say with a grin. 'My accessories are jerk vest and pads, not sunglasses.'

'Whatever you say,' she says with a laugh. Before I know what's happening, she puts her arms around my neck and whispers in my ear. 'I'm glad you got one too.'

I freeze. Her hair smells so good.

'Did you just sniff me?' she says, jumping back.

Oh God. Did I?

'No,' I say.

Blake bursts out laughing.

'I have a cold,' I say, quickly pretending to sneeze.

'That has got to be the worst fake sneeze known to mankind. Maybe you should go back to drama school,' says Blake. Then a knowing expression fills his face and he smiles wickedly.

'I'll see you later,' I say, darting into my room.

Why would I smell her hair?

Then my chest tightens. I always thought she was pretty, but do I like her? I mean—really, really like her?

More importantly—does Blake know?

CHAPTER 22

I make my way to the buffet at 5 o'clock the next morning. There's no way I can face Mawi or Blake. The staff are only just putting out breakfast, and so I grab bananas and pastries before heading to the cliffside where I'm doing today's stunt. To my surprise Novak and Alistair are already there, their backs to me, looking out to sea. I'm downwind of the strong sea breeze and their voices carry towards me.

'It's done,' says Alistair. 'It will affect him soon.'

'How much did you give him?' says Novak.

'Enough to kill him.'

I stop walking. What the hell are they talking about? Suddenly in my mind I see the cameraman from yesterday trailing blood. For the hundredth time, I wish Anna were still here. Something tells me I shouldn't be. I step backward, tripping over a tree root. Alistair spins round and my heart jolts. He has a black eye and his shoulder's bleeding.

'What are you doing up so early?' he calls to me, his face like thunder.

Novak whisks around too.

I tuck my hand behind my ear and shout, 'What are you saying? I can't hear you over the wind and sea.'

Alistair's face lightens a little, and I force myself to walk closer.

'I asked you why you're up so early.'

'I wanted to check out the jump for today.'

Novak beams. 'Finn, you are such a thorough stunt double.'

But Alistair's face turns thunderous again. 'You're jumping from here to the sea?'

'Yeah.'

'Are you serious? Have you seen what it's like?'

'No,' I say uneasily. I step alongside him, and gulp. It's not only deep, there are jagged rocks sticking out all over the place, the waves crashing down on them.

'I wouldn't have asked him to do it, if I didn't think he could. Do you think I want my special stunt double injured?' says Novak.

Special stunt double?

'I'll be fine,' I say, trying to sound braver than I feel.

'Do you mind if we have a chat in private?' Alistair grabs my shoulder, pulling me away, before Novak has a chance to speak. 'Do you know what's interesting about this little spot?' he says.

'No,' I say, backing away from his grip. He looks even more deranged than usual.

'This is where Anna hurt herself. She was lucky she only broke her leg.'

'It is?' I whisper.

'Yes!' Then he shakes his head. 'You think you're Novak's special stunt double? She's only using you because you're a kid too scared to say no.'

'I'm not scared.'

He snorts. 'Perhaps you're not. Perhaps you're just mad. But I think you'd rather kill yourself than let her down. And she knows that.' He looks at me urgently. Suddenly not crazy or angry, but . . . desperate. 'You don't have to do this.'

'I've jumped into the sea before,' I say.

'You won't change your mind?'

I glance at Novak. She's watching us carefully. 'No,' I say.

'Suit yourself. But I'm not going to watch, I'm going to bed. I didn't get much sleep last night.'

'What happened to your face?' I say, the words slipping out.

'I couldn't say no to Novak either. Watch yourself, Finn.'

A few hours later, I'm wearing swimming shorts, and the crew are setting up. There are cranes dangling off the cliff edge, so the cameras can follow my every move. We're going straight to tape—no rehearsals this time—and just one take. I think I can thank Alistair for that.

Conner looks nervous. 'Alistair said he didn't want to watch you die, so I'm here.'

'Thanks for the confidence boost,' I reply.

He smiles, but I can tell it's fake.

'I'm not sure why we got you a jerk vest. You never wear it.'

'It's only a jump. I've been working it out. If I land in the sea at that point there,' I point to a space between a group of rocks, 'I'll be fine.'

'I'm thinking Alistair had the right idea. I don't want to watch you die either. But I'll be down on the beach, next to the paramedic.' Conner starts walking over to the narrow stone steps leading to the shore.

'Again—thanks for the confidence boost,' I call.

His shoulders rise up and down, and I can tell he's laughing. He can't be that worried.

The sea seems even rougher than this morning, the waves exploding onto the rocks. I take deep calming breaths of salty sea air . . . except they're not that calming. *Come on—I can do this.* I've jumped into swimming pools from really high diving boards. It's just the same . . . isn't it?

127

'Cameras ready? Lights ready? Sound ready? Action!' booms a voice through a megaphone.

I bend my legs and jump, except my feet don't move.

'Is everything okay?' calls the AD.

No! I don't want to do this. But somehow I force my hand into a thumbs up.

'Cameras ready? Lights ready? Sound ready? Action!' booms a voice.

It's now or never. Clenching my fists, I leap over the edge. Salt flies up my nose. Spray crashes onto my face and I slam my eyes shut, as I hit the water. It's not cold, but the current is strong. It pushes me, banging my body against a giant rock, but I can use that as a kick board. Pushing off, I swim through the crashing waves, finding the narrow alleyway of clear water. I swim harder than I've ever done before, until I reach the rocky shore.

'And cut!'

'Brilliant,' yells Conner.

I can't believe I did it.

I tread carefully over jagged rocks, my toes curling every time I hit a loose stone. Fortunately the steps to the top of the cliff are far smoother, but there are loads of them. I'm sweating by the time I reach the top.

'That was fabulous,' cries Novak, striding towards me.

The crew stomp and cheer.

'You are freaking mad,' says one of the cameramen. 'That was one of the most awesome things I've ever seen.'

'You were amazing,' cries Mawi. 'We watched it on playback on the camera.'

'Thanks,' I mutter, peering at her out of the corner of my eyes. Does she remember yesterday? I catch a glimpse of Blake. While everyone's still cheering, his arms are folded, and his lip curled. He looks . . . jealous?

Novak claps her hands. 'We must do another take.'

'What? I thought we were only doing one.'

'There's been a change of plan. And this time, you won't be alone,' says Novak. 'Mawi's doing it with you. You need to hold her hand and jump off the top together.'

'She's jumping too? But Anna—'

'Mawi has you to talk her through it, and you'll be holding her hand. I should have brought you with Anna. That was my mistake.'

'But—'

'Girls are just as capable as boys, aren't they Mawi?'

'Absolutely,' she says.

'Finn, you need to go back to hair, make-up, and wardrobe. I need you to start off dry.'

*

An hour later, Mawi and I stand at the edge of the cliff top. Somehow it seems even higher now she's jumping too. I still can't look her in the face. Gazing at the sea, I tell her where to aim for and what to do when we get down there.

'Any questions?' I say finally.

'Do we have to do it?' she whispers.

I look at her sharply. Her face is clammy, and slightly green.

'You can refuse.'

'You wouldn't.' She gives herself a shake and says, 'I'll be fine.'

I take her hand. 'I won't let anything happen to you, I promise. You ready?'

'I guess.'

I lift my other hand in a thumbs up.

'Lights, camera, action.'

We leap over the edge. I feel her hand pull away, and I grip onto it harder. The wind and spray envelop us, before we plunge into the clear patch of water. Together we scramble to get back to the surface, when Mawi's hand jerks away. I open my eyes. Her arms start flailing; she kicks wildly. I try to grab her, when she grabs me instead. One arm around my neck the other around my body. Her legs still thrashing. I need to breathe, but she tugs us deeper.

The current slams us towards a rock.

I can't get free to swim.

CHAPTER

23

Mawi crashes into a rock. Her arms float off me and she starts to drop. I'm free ... but I can't leave her. Darting lower, my lungs feel like bursting. I wrap one arm around her middle, but she feels floppy. How bad did she hit her head? Then I see red seep into the water. She's cut!

Grabbing her under the chin, I kick as hard as I can, propelling us closer and closer to the surface. At last, we burst through. I take a massive gulp of air, before releasing my arm from round her middle. With her chin still cupped in my hand, I lie on my back. I swim backstroke with only one arm, glancing behind me every so often, making sure we're not heading for rocks. The water gets shallower.

'You can let go. I've got her.'

Conner's waded through the sea. I unravel my fingers and he whisks her into his arms. I realize I can stand. As if in a trance I follow them onto the rocky beach, not noticing the pebbles jabbing into my feet.

Mawi, please be okay!

The paramedic swoops towards her. He lays her sideways and she coughs. Water spurts out of her mouth and her eyes open.

Thank God!

She grabs hold of the paramedic's arm and says, 'Did we get the shot?'

Conner, the paramedic, and I burst out laughing.

'Yeah, we got it,' I say, falling backwards on to the rocks. Whether we have or not, there's no way on earth we're redoing that take!

The paramedic puts a bandage around Mawi's head, and now we're out of the water, I don't think she's that hurt. Definitely shocked. Conner takes her back to her room, while the paramedic checks me over. I'm absolutely fine, but Novak makes me drink a hot chocolate before I'm allowed back to my room. As I head along our floor, Mawi's door swings open. 'You saved my life!'

I have to smile. She has a massive chocolate moustache.

'You had a hot chocolate too,' I say.

'How do you—? Oh.' She wipes her mouth with the back of her hand and laughs. 'You saved my life,' she says again.

'No I didn't. Conner and the others were there. Someone would have got you out.'

'But they didn't. You did. Conner told me all about it.'

'Really—it was nothing,' I say.

'What is going on?' says Blake, opening his door. 'I'm trying to rehearse. Can you—what happened to your head?'

'Weren't you there? Didn't you see Mawi jump?' I say.

'I left after your first shot,' he says, not taking his eyes off Mawi. 'What happened?'

'I hit my head on the rocks in the water,' says Mawi, before launching into a heroic tale. I have to admit, she makes me sound great.

Blake's eyebrows rise. He looks at me for a second. Then suddenly leans towards her.

'How's your head now?' he asks, gently stroking her bandage.

She gasps and I think she actually trembles. 'It's— *erm*—it's . . . '

'The reason I ask,' Blake pauses and gives her one of his smouldering smiles, the ones he normally saves for the film, 'I was hoping we could practise our lines together. Just you and me.'

'Really?' whispers Mawi. 'Now?'

'Only if you feel well enough.'

Mawi grins as if she's won the lottery. 'I'd love to.'

'Great.' They disappear off into his room.

'I guess I'll see you later then,' I snap.

How did that happen? I went from being her hero to invisible in less than 30 seconds. I don't think I've ever hated Blake as much as I do right now.

I trudge back to my room, suddenly feeling exhausted. I guess the adrenalin's worn off. I flop onto my bed and within minutes I'm fast asleep.

∗

I open my eyes to light streaming in through the windows. I must have forgotten to close the curtains. I'm still wearing the clothes from yesterday, and the last thing I remember was collapsing on my bed—but that was late afternoon. I didn't even have dinner. I glance at my watch.

That can't be right.

I turn to the clock on my bedside table. What the—? They both say the same thing—but it can't be ten. I was supposed to be in a stunt at nine. Truck should have woken me. Or Mawi and Blake . . . unless the star couple don't want me around.

I jump in and out of the shower, shove on some clothes, and race down the stairs. Hopefully they'll still have some breakfast set out in the restaurant and I can grab a bite before heading to the beach where we're filming again. At the thought of food I speed up even more.

I burst into the restaurant. It's completely empty. No film crew, no staff, and no food. There's nothing on the buffet table, not even crumbs or empty glasses. I can't believe I missed it. And where is everyone? Are they at the beach?

I hurry out of the hotel, not meeting gardeners, cleaners, or guests like I normally do. I can only hear screeches of insects and animals; no human voices. When I reach the beach, I find it empty too. What is going on? I feel the panic rising. Then I think of Reception—there's always someone there.

I rush back to the hotel, through the restaurant and into the lobby. I don't believe it, there's no one here either. Heading straight for the reception desk, I slam the bell, but the sound just echoes in the silence of the room. No one comes. It's like I'm in a horror film, where everyone's snatched in the night . . .

Suddenly I hear running footsteps. My eyes dart to the direction of the noise. Is someone coming to snatch me too?

CHAPTER
24

I'm ready to run, when Mawi sprints into the lobby. Muscles I didn't even know I was tensing, relax. Her face fills with relief too.

'You're here,' she gasps. 'Have you seen anyone else?'

I shake my head.

'Not even Blake?'

That figures. Out of everyone she's thinking of him.

'I've no idea where anyone is. I woke up this morning and—' My voice cracks.

'It's strange, isn't it?'

'It's beyond freaky.'

'I was coming here to call my parents.'

The telephone—of course! 'Yeah, that's why I'm here

too,' I lie.

'Do you think we can use the phone without permission?'

I almost laugh. 'There's no one here to stop us.'

We walk behind the desk. Mawi reaches her hand toward the phone, then hesitates. I pick it up, and nearly cry with relief. There's a dial tone. For a moment, I thought we'd have no phone line or electricity or anything. I've obviously watched too many horror films.

'What's your parents' number?' I ask.

'I'll do it,' she says, taking it from me.

'Ah, children, you're here.'

We spin around at the familiar voice.

'Novak!' I cry.

She walks towards us, her arms outstretched. 'I've been looking for you everywhere.'

'I was just about to ring my parents,' says Mawi, holding up the receiver.

'Oh goodness—you don't need to do that. Put the phone down,' says Novak. She smiles warmly as Mawi hangs up. 'You must have both been terrified. How clever of you to think to ring Mawi's parents. I'm assuming that was your idea,' she says, looking at me.

'No, it was Mawi's.'

Novak jerks her head back in surprise, then clasps her hand to her chest. 'Is that true? Didn't I choose well?'

Mawi and I look at each other. What is she talking about?

'I hoped to catch you on your floor when you woke up, but I got waylaid. I wanted to explain what's going on.'

'What is going on?' says Mawi.

'Where is everyone?' I ask.

'They are at a different hotel, about five miles from here. They left last night. I organized it.'

'Even the staff?' says Mawi.

Novak shakes her head. 'I gave them a couple of days off, with full pay of course.'

'But why?' This doesn't feel right.

'And that is the important question. Please, come with me.'

We follow her out of the lobby, down a few paths until we reach the clearing where the climbing wall was. It's gone, replaced by a metal cage with a mechanical Ropen inside, the one twice my size from the studio back in England.

'This fake Ropen is such a disappointment, is it not? It breaks so easily,' says Novak, and my eyes fall to the floor. I know she's thinking about the foot. 'Wouldn't it be wonderful if the real thing existed? Then I wouldn't have to use CGI. And if it did exist, wouldn't it be wonderful if we could use her in the film?'

'Her? I always thought of it as a him,' I say.

'She's definitely a her,' says Novak, squeezing her arm between the bars of the cage and stroking the metal creature. 'Imagine my delight when I discovered the Ropen does exist. She is alive and well, living off an island close to here.'

138

What???

'Are you for real? She's not a myth?' I turn to Mawi, who's looking at Novak as if she's grown five heads.

'She is very real,' says Novak.

'Is she immortal?' I ask.

Novak pulls out her arm. 'Now that part is made up—for my film. Mawi, surely you have heard about her sightings?'

'I've heard about them, but never believed them. Only my great-uncle thought they were true. Dad said they're hallucinations or mistakes. He says people see giant bats.'

'Then your papa is wrong.'

Mawi's mouth drops open.

'Unless you're saying I am wrong,' says Novak, smiling a little too sweetly. 'I sent some men to get her for me. Unfortunately they came back empty-handed.'

'Truck and Alistair,' I say, the names slipping out.

'They told you?' Novak's eyes flash.

'No,' I say, quickly, not wanting to get them into trouble. 'Anna and I saw them with some other men. They were limping. Is the creature dangerous?'

'When did you see them?'

I kick a stone on the floor.

'When did you see them?' she repeats.

'We snuck out at night, about a week and a half ago,' I mumble.

Novak puts her arm around my waist, and I think of a Papuan death adder. I force myself not to move.

'And this is why you are the perfect boy. You break rules to do whatever you want,' she says. 'And this is why you are going to bring me back the Ropen.'

Whoa! I twist out of her grasp.

'The pair of you are going to the island to bring me back my creature. Oh don't look so worried. You don't have to fly on her back. You will catch her in a net and my men will pick her up. Then she can be in my film.'

'Are you mad?' Again the words slip out.

'She will be the star of *The Ropen's Revenge.*' Novak looks into the distance. 'And when I win my Oscar, I will thank you two for the part you played—not just as actors and stunt doubles, but for helping me realize my dream.'

'Which island is she on?' says Mawi.

'Gamboi Island.'

Mawi shakes her head and steps backwards. 'I can't go there. The tribe will kill me.'

'No, they will listen to you. You have their blood running through your veins. Your great-grandpapa was one of them. I know you know their language. It is why I hired you.'

'You hired me because of this?' says Mawi, wrapping her arms around her body.

'Alistair discovered I needed someone who speaks their language.'

Her words hit me like a wrecking ball. Did she get rid of Anna on purpose? I think of the note.

'My great-grandfather would have told my granddad

or my mother about the Ropen. But they don't believe in it, so he can't have done.'

'I imagine your great-grandpapa never mentioned her because he was sworn to secrecy, like so many Gamboins. Although I'm wondering whether he did tell your great-uncle.'

I scrape my hand through my hair. 'If she does exist, can't you just buy the Ropen? Offer them gold or whatever else they want.'

'Do you think I haven't thought of that? According to their culture, the Ropen is a powerful ally. They will not relinquish her.'

'But why are you using me?' I ask. 'Surely there are others who are better.'

'Don't put yourself down, Finn. You never give up. You are physically strong and resourceful.'

The world is crashing down. 'Is this why you hired me? You never wanted me as a stunt double?'

'I did. I do. But you are more important than a mere stunt boy. *You* will help me get the Ropen. This is your destiny.'

'What if I say no?'

'You won't.' Novak smiles. 'Because if you do, your mama will die.'

CHAPTER 25

If anyone else threatened my mum, I would think they were joking. But this is Novak. She doesn't joke.

As if in a trance, I follow her to a large warehouse, close to where I tried to dump the baby snake.

Mawi keeps glancing at me. 'Are you okay?' she whispers.

How am I supposed to answer that?

Novak holds the door open for us. Dreading what I'll find, I step inside. It's an enormous empty space, apart from one section, an inner room with four walls made entirely out of glass. Conner and a cameraman are inside, sitting on a sofa, fiddling with a microphone. There's also a TV and three dolls on a coffee table. I recognize them straight away. Blake, Mawi, and me, taken out of their boxes.

'Where's Mum?' I ask.

'You thought your mama was here?' says Novak, with a laugh. 'She's still in England.'

'Then what—'

'All will be revealed.'

Conner and the cameraman suddenly notice us. They grin and wave. Their mouths move, but I can't hear a thing. Cold envelops my body. Is Conner in on this, like Alistair and Truck? But he's my friend. . .

Moving closer to one of the glass walls, Novak says, 'The room is completely soundproof. We can't hear them. They can't hear us.' She pulls a remote control out of her pocket, and presses a button. 'I would like you to watch the dolls.'

Suddenly the eyes of the action figures glow bright red. Like pinprick lasers.

What the . . . ?

Mawi's hand grasps mine.

Conner and the cameraman stand up, walk over to the dolls, and then look back at us. Conner mouths, 'What's going on?'

I shrug.

Then he begins to cough. So does the cameraman. They grab their throats, their bodies jerk. They collapse to the floor, rolling about, their mouths opening and shutting like fish out of water.

143

'What's happening?' I shout.

'The dolls are filled with a poisonous gas,' says Novak, calmly.

Ripping my hand out of Mawi's grasp, I run around the glass walls, searching for a door. At last I spot a handle and pull, but the door remains stuck fast.

'It's locked,' says Novak.

'How can you do this? Give me the remote.'

I charge towards her. She's so small, I'll wrestle it from her. Then two thick arms wrap around me.

'Alistair,' I shout, squirming frantically, making no impact whatsoever. 'Conner's your friend.'

'Sometimes sacrifices have to be made,' says Alistair stiffly.

Mawi lunges for Novak. Alistair releases one arm from around me and grabs her shoulder, pinching tight. Mawi squeals, dropping to the ground. With only one arm, he's got less of a grip around me. I elbow him hard in the chest then spin, kicking him in the neck. He stumbles backwards. I kick again and he grabs my foot.

'Don't injure him. I need him,' yells Novak.

Grimacing, Alistair pulls me into a tight grip again and I know he won't make the same mistake twice.

Mawi scrambles to her feet, and lunges for Novak again.

'You're too late,' says Novak.

Mawi turns, her eyes widening. She slams her hands onto the glass. The figures inside lie still.

My stomach lurches and I throw up on Alistair's foot. He leaps backwards, releasing me. I want to hit him again—and Novak—but I feel dizzy, sick, weak. Clutching my stomach, I look the other way as Alistair unlocks the glass door. There's grunting and shuffling. By the time I return my gaze, the room is empty.

'It was very noble of you both to try to save them,' says Novak, 'but there was nothing you could do. Once the gas hits your lungs, you're dead.'

'Why did you do that?' whispers Mawi, her face clammy.

I look around the room. Alistair's not back yet. This is our chance. There's no way Novak can overpower us. Mawi and I should run. The phones are still working, and we can call the police.

I grab Mawi's arm, vaguely aware of Novak pointing the remote at the glass room again.

'We have to go,' I hiss into her ear.

She looks at me, her eyes clearing. We run for the door, when Novak's voice rings out loud and clear.

'You will want to see this.'

'No, we won't,' I shout, over my shoulder.

Then my blood freezes. The TV in the glass room is now on. I drop Mawi's hand, and without taking my eyes off the screen, walk slowly back to the glass room. Somehow I'm staring at my lounge back in England. Mum's put the action figure of me on the mantelpiece. She's sitting on the sofa, reading a book, glancing over at my action man ever so often. The massive banner MY SON THE SUPERSTAR still hangs across the wall.

'Who's that?' says Mawi.

To my surprise she's beside me. I thought she would have bolted.

'My mum,' I whisper, and she grabs my hand again.

'Your mama is so proud of you,' says Novak. 'Think of all the sacrifices she made during her life to get you in a film.'

'How can we see her? How can we see the action figure?' I ask, my heart trying to break free from its ribcage.

'When my men delivered the doll, they also snuck in a camera,' says Novak.

'You bugged my house? You put poisonous gas in my lounge?' I want to punch her lights out.

She presses the remote and the image changes to another room. This time there are bunk beds and Mawi's doll is on the windowsill.

'That's my sisters' room,' she whimpers, falling to her knees.

'They were most insistent the doll went in there,' says Novak. Then her eyes harden. 'Now listen to me the pair of you. You will go to Gamboi, you will capture the Ropen, or I will activate the dolls.'

For a moment there's silence. I can't speak. I don't think Mawi can either. Then I look at the three action figures. 'Is Blake coming too?'

'Oh no,' says Novak. 'He would be a liability.'

I wait for Mawi to correct her, but she's still gazing at the image of her sisters' bedroom.

'Blake would slow you down. He is not fit for such an important job. You are the chosen one,' she adds, looking at me expectantly.

Am I supposed to be pleased?

'However, I have found a use for a Blake doll.'

She hits the remote and the screen changes to a hospital room with Anna lying on a bed, her leg strung up in a cast. A Rio doll is on the windowsill. Anna's obviously got to it. She's drawn a moustache, acne, and devil horns. She's tried to make it look goofy, but right now, I've never seen anything scarier in my life.

I open and close my fists. Novak can't get away with this. Alistair's still not returned . . . and Novak is so small.

I charge towards her, ready to rugby-tackle, kick, I don't know what. But she leaps out of the way and yells, 'They'll die if I'm hurt.'

I stop mid-jump.

'I have friends in England, Papua, America. If they don't hear from me every day, they know to activate the dolls.'

'We'll call the police,' says Mawi, jumping to her feet, her eyes flashing.

Novak chucks her palms out in front. 'Then I won't call my friends. The police can't make me and they will not know where they are.'

I feel like the world is collapsing at my feet.

'All because you want a real life Ropen for a film?' I say, fighting back tears.

'Movies are important,' says Novak. 'After people have died, movies remain. They are our history. And you and me—we will go down in history.'

'You're a monster,' cries Mawi.

'I am a director,' says Novak.

'You killed Conner,' I hiss. 'You're a murderer. And for what? A mythological creature? You're freaking mad!'

Novak's nostrils flare and she switches off the TV. 'I think you are focusing far too much on the past. We need to focus on the future. And if you want any future, you will do what I say.'

CHAPTER 26

'I think you have everything you need. I packed it myself,' says Alistair, pointing at the rucksack. 'They're special waterproof bags.'

Mawi, Alistair, and I are back in the lobby. I don't know where Novak is. I drop to my knees and open the bag. Penknife, compass, energy bars, water, spare clothes. Mawi's going through hers too, sobbing quietly.

'Why are you doing this?' I ask, my voice cracking as I look up at Alistair.

'I tried to get rid of you. I told you to fail,' he says.

'I thought you didn't want me doing stunts.'

'I didn't give a rat's bum about the stunts. I didn't want you involved in any of this. My girlfriend was in line for the job, but I managed to get her off the hook. I told Novak to find another stunt double. I had no idea she'd find a child.' He scrapes his hands through his hair. 'And Kid, every time you succeeded without being rigged to something, you made Novak even more convinced you were the best person for the job.'

'Don't call me Kid,' I say, leaping to my feet. 'That's Conner's name for me.'

Alistair's face is pinched. 'If you'd failed, then Conner would be alive.'

'Seriously? You're trying to blame me for murdering Conner? Hey—if that makes you feel better.'

He stands over me, his fists clenched. One punch from him and I'd be out cold. That's it . . . That's what I need him to do . . .

'Don't you dare go to Gamboi yourself? Or are you too scared?' I taunt.

The vein on his temple pulses. 'I tried, but the tribe wouldn't let me in. I couldn't speak their language. They didn't trust me.'

'Wonder why?' I snap.

'Boys, boys, stop fighting,' says Novak, reappearing with a rolled up piece of paper in her hands. 'Finn, save your aggression for the jungle—you'll need it. And Mawi, stop snivelling. It's getting tiresome. I don't want to have to make you.'

A sob explodes from her and Novak nods at Alistair. 'If you know what's good for you, you'll stop,' he snarls, moving towards her.

Mawi clamps her mouth shut, and looks at me with such fear.

'Let me go on my own. I can get the Ropen without her. She'll hold me back,' I say.

'That is not very kind. Mawi is capable. And you need her once you get to the tribe.' Novak hands the rolled up paper to Alistair. 'Now Mawi and I need to discuss her role, while you must go over the map with Finn.' She turns to me. 'I'm afraid the map is incomplete. We only know the Gamboi village from the sky.'

'Why's it incomplete?' I say, the words tasting bitter. I think I know the answer.

'My men didn't make it inside. They got to the perimeter but were then . . . waylaid.'

Yep—that's what I guessed. 'So you think we can get further than grown men?'

'I have faith in you, Finn. It's about time you did too.'

✳

It takes about an hour for Alistair to go over the map, and explain how we're going to trap the Ropen. He shows me the journey to the tribe, but knows nothing about their village—where they sleep, where they eat, where they keep the creature.

'So it wasn't the Ropen that attacked you?' I say.

'How do you know we were attacked?'

'Anna and I saw you come back. Truck was limping.'

151

Alistair raises his eyebrows. 'Yet you stayed?' He shakes his head. 'It wasn't the Ropen. I've never seen her.'

'But she definitely exists?'

'For all our sakes I hope so. It was the tribe who attacked us. They're dangerous.'

'So let me get this straight. According to your map, the land is dangerous with crocodiles, steep cliffs. Now you're telling me the tribe is dangerous. And for all we know the Ropen might not even exist.'

'I think that sums it up. Now remember, once you've caught her, send up the flares. You'll have about five minutes to get to the top of the cliff where we'll collect you.'

Suddenly it occurs to me—if we catch the Ropen, but don't get back, Novak can still make her film. She's already replaced Anna. She can replace Mawi and me too.

'Will you definitely be there?' I say.

'I will,' says Alistair. 'I will do anything in my power to not leave you behind.'

'You know you could stop this. You're big enough to overpower Novak.'

Alistair closes his eyes. 'Finn, you're not the only one she's threatening. I have family too. She's been planning this for months. You saw the snakes on the plane. Who knows what else she's set up.' He opens his eyes again. 'Let's just do what we have to do.'

I stuff the map into the front pocket of my rucksack

and hoist the bag onto my shoulders. In silence, Alistair and I walk out of the hotel, but as we reach the helipad, I stop, my feet refusing to go on.

'Tell me Novak's not flying,' I say.

The helicopter from the airport stands in the middle of the grass. Novak and Mawi lean against it. Mawi looks like she wants to be sick.

'I'm flying. We want to get you there in one piece,' says Alistair.

'You okay?' I say to Mawi, as soon as we approach them, but she doesn't answer.

'Mawi will be fine. She knows exactly what she has to do,' says Novak. 'Has Alistair told you about the venom?'

'Venom?' My legs weaken. I don't think I can take much more.

'Alistair and his men shot the leader of the Gamboi tribe with darts covered in adder venom from England. As there is no antidote here, they—'

'So that's why you brought them,' I exclaim. 'They're not props.'

'I needed fresh venom. Unfortunately they have antidotes for their own Papuan death adders here, otherwise I could have used those.'

'You killed their leader?'

'He's not dead yet. He will be if Mawi doesn't give him the antidote. She is going to gain the tribe's trust by making him better.'

'For the hundredth time—how am I supposed to

gain their trust?' says Mawi. 'My great-grandfather had to leave. He was exiled. He was told that no member of his family can ever return, otherwise they'll die.'

Oh God!

'You're an actress. Act. Persuade them you are trustworthy,' says Novak. '*Once* you have gained their trust, they will show you where the Ropen is. And at night, the pair of you will catch her.'

'That's the plan?' I say.

'It is foolproof, is it not?'

That isn't quite what I'm thinking!

Alistair opens the helicopter door, when I hear a shout:

'I knew it. You're trying to push me out of the film. Use Finn instead of me.'

I turn to see Blake running towards us. My heart leaps. Who brought him here? Are they nearby? 'Help us!' I mouth from behind Novak's back.

'My father will be hearing about this,' yells Blake.

'Help us!' I mouth again.

Novak's face turns pale. 'Blake, we are not filming anything. Mawi and Finn are doing a little favour for me.' She steps towards him. 'Why are you here? Who brought you?'

'One of the stuntmen mentioned you were all still at this hotel, and straight away I guessed what was happening. I got a seaplane to drop me off.'

'I didn't hear one,' says Novak.

'So?'

'Is the pilot still here?' says Novak.

'No, he left,' say Blake looking smug. 'I'm all alone. You're stuck with me.'

My heart drops faster than a speeding poisonous dart.

CHAPTER 27

Why did you tell her we were all alone?

'You look so disappointed,' Blake says to me, with a sneer. 'I'm sorry to spoil your fun but Rio is my role.'

'Finn is not taking your role,' says Novak.

'Should I call my dad now? Tell him what's going on,' says Blake.

'Yes,' I say quickly. 'Call him up.'

Novak's eyes flicker between Blake and me. Then she lifts her hands into the air. 'Okay, I give up. Blake, you can go too.'

'But you said he was a liability,' I blurt.

'A liability?' Blake's face reddens. 'I put everything

into Rio. I practise my lines all night, I—'

'Get into the helicopter, Blake, and prove yourself,' says Novak.

Her tone shuts us all up. Blake climbs in first, followed by Mawi, then me.

'What if something happens to him?' says Alistair. 'He's the star. His dad is . . . '

'Finn will look after him. He will bring him back or . . . ' She looks at me and raises her eyebrows.

Oh great!

'What do you mean he'll look after me?' says Blake. 'I don't need—'

'Finn, you have three days or the dolls will be activated. We can't set back filming too much,' says Novak, before slamming the door to the helicopter.

Alistair climbs into the front and Novak walks away.

'Where's Novak going?' says Blake, looking out the window. At last he's beginning to look nervous. 'Why isn't she getting in the front?'

'You asked to come,' I say, leaning my head against the window.

The rotor blades start whirring and soon we rise into the air. It's like I'm dreaming, watching myself sitting in the helicopter. Three days! My brain keeps going back to the television screen with Mum in the lounge glancing at my action figure. Somewhere in the background, I'm aware of Blake hammering us with questions. I think we're all ignoring him. I can't fail, but how the hell am

I supposed to travel across an island, release the Ropen when grown men can't? Grown men like Alistair and Truck.

We soar over brilliant blue sea, over islands that look like mountains of broccoli. At any other time I'd think they were spectacular, but right now they look dangerous, unknown. Finally Alistair begins to descend to a narrow stretch of beach. He's dropping us at the far end of Gamboi, nowhere near the tribe, so we don't spook them or alert them of our arrival. I just hope no members are out on the beach today. Sand swirls in the air as we land, obscuring the rainforest behind.

Blake's looking out the window, frowning. 'Are the film crew already here?'

'They're not coming. Novak wasn't lying when she said we're not filming,' I say.

'Are we rehearsing then?'

'We're doing real life.'

Alistair jumps out of the helicopter and whisks open the back door.

'Before you get out, all of you put this on. And use lots.' He throws me a spray—insect repellent. 'People think it's the big animals that are dangerous in the jungle, but it's the thousands of tiny creatures you have to worry about. They eat you alive.'

'You're not making me feel better,' I say, spraying every part of my skin that's on show. 'I don't suppose you have a Blake repellent too?'

Glaring at me, Blake covers himself, and Mawi does the same.

'It's time to get out,' says Alistair, holding the door even wider.

There's no option. Grabbing my bag, I climb out first and the others follow.

'I want to know what's going on,' says Blake.

'Finn will explain everything when I've gone,' says Alistair.

'Why's it all Finn, Finn, Finn? Is he the bleeding oracle?' Then he pauses. 'Aren't you staying?'

'Nothing would make me stay on this island,' says Alistair.

I look at him in horror.

'Perhaps I shouldn't have said that.'

'You think?' I snap.

'I'm not staying here with just these two,' says Blake. 'Take me back on the helicopter.'

'You asked to come remember,' says Alistair.

'Granddad told me about the Gamboi tribe,' says Mawi, suddenly. 'He says they never forget. They're loyal to those they love, but will kill those they hate. And they hated my great-grandfather.'

'What did he do?' I say.

'I don't know. No one would ever tell me.'

'I've got to go,' says Alistair. 'I wouldn't stay out in the open if I were you.'

'You can't leave us here,' says Blake.

I step towards the helicopter when Alistair says, 'Think of the dolls. Think of your mum.'

I freeze, watching him climb back into the aircraft.

'It's going to be windy. Get out of here,' he calls.

Mawi and I grab our bags and together with Blake, we run for the rainforest. Seconds later, the blades start whirring, whipping sand everywhere. From behind a tree, we watch the helicopter rise through the cloudy air, until it becomes a mere dot in the sky. Even though the heat is soaring, cold clings to my body. Alistair left us.

'They'll hate me,' whispers Mawi.

'For the love of God, will someone tell me what is going on?' says Blake. 'We've just been stranded in the middle of nowhere. Is this some sort of documentary or am I being pranked or—'

I tell Blake everything. He doesn't interrupt, and after I finish, there's silence.

He leans against a tree, and at last he says, 'Are you being serious? Is this for real?'

'Bet you wish you'd never left the other hotel now,' I say.

He gulps, and looks like he wants to vomit.

'At least your parents are safe.'

'But they're not. I sent the Rio doll to my dad. One of the crew was going home yesterday, and he's giving it to Dad today. I was proud of it. Thought he'd be proud of it too.'

Oh God!

'Do you think it's got poisonous gas in it?' he whispers.

'I don't know,' I say softly.

Blake slides down the tree, his head falling into his hands. I swallow hard. This all seems so hopeless. But we can't stay here. We have three days. I take the map and penknife out of my bag.

'Alistair gave me instructions,' I say.

CHAPTER 28

Mawi and I chuck the rucksacks over our shoulders, and I stare at Blake's empty back. Of course! Since he didn't know he was coming, he doesn't have a bag, but that means he doesn't have any supplies either. We're going to have to share. Great! Right now I have other things to worry about though. We have to go uphill through dense rainforest without any pathways or tourist trails.

Mawi and I try to slice through ferns and thick green leaves with penknives. Couldn't Alistair have given us machetes? The trees are so tall, only sprinkles of light reach us. We break through cobwebs, climb over roots, and dodge vines, while waving away insects on a mission for our blood. I don't think they read the label on Alistair's spray. The air is thick, humid. Layers of sweat coat my body and I miss the sea breeze. It even smells hot. Birds and other creatures squawk, hiss, and click. The leaves rustle above and I try not to think about Papuan death snakes and whatever else might be around.

'Couldn't he have dropped us off at the top?' whines Blake.

'We might have been seen.'

'Who cares if we're seen if we die from exhaustion?'

Higher and higher we go. My thighs burn. We pass fragrant exotic flowers that Mum would love. Thinking about her is what keeps me going. At long last, the ground seems to flatten, and even though it's still covered in jungle, we're surely near the top.

I drop my bag and sit on the edge of a large rock. 'We should rest.'

'Finally,' says Blake.

I grab some energy bars and throw one to each of them. Ripping open my packet, I stuff the granola into my mouth. Mawi brings out a bottle of water, takes a few sips, before handing it to Blake. He starts gulping.

'Whoa!' I yelp. 'That's got to last.'

Reluctantly, he passes over the bottle. I swirl one sip of water round my mouth before giving it back to Mawi.

'What if we run out?' says Blake.

'There should be natural springs around here,' says Mawi.

I look at her in surprise. 'Have you trekked through the jungle before?'

'I'm from round here, of course I have. Not on this island though. I'm not allowed. My family's not allowed.'

A shiver goes down my back.

Mawi takes a small bite of energy bar before putting it into her pocket. Yeah, she knows what she's doing. Perhaps she should be in charge.

We look at the map and I show them the route Novak planned for us.

'She wants us to do that in one day?' says Blake.

'Two,' I say. 'There's a cave halfway down the river where Alistair left us food and sleeping bags. Also a bag with the stuff for trapping the Ropen.'

'What if someone else finds it?' says Mawi.

'Let's hope they don't.'

She glances down at her watch. 'We only have about three hours before it gets dark. We should get going.'

I stand up, when the leaves crash around us. Something's hurtling through the trees. I get ready to run, when there's a thud. A creature about the size of a chicken lands in front of us. It's hunched like a kangaroo, but furrier, with a kind of mouse-lemur face. It's staring at us as much as we are staring at it.

'A tree kangaroo,' whispers Mawi.

She holds out some of her energy bar and the creature's nostrils flare.

'Go on,' she says softly, dropping to one knee.

The creature sniffs again. Then bounds forward in one jump, grabs the piece of granola, and scarpers back into the jungle.

'That was amazing,' I say.

Mawi's eyes gleam. 'I think it's a good omen. I think we'll be all right.'

'Tree kangaroos bring good luck?'

'Yeah, let's say they do.'

'I can't believe you just did that,' says Blake. 'I could have eaten it. You wasted it on a monkey.'

'It wasn't a monkey,' I say, rolling my eyes. I glance at Mawi, hoping she'll do the same, but she breaks off more of the energy bar and hands it to Blake.

He grabs it.

'Are you going to bound into the jungle too?' I ask.

Blake scowls, while Mawi tries not to laugh.

I pull the compass from the front pocket of my bag and we head north. Mawi takes the lead, and I watch her navigate the forest floor with ease. Blake just grumbles behind.

'You know—if you stopped moaning, you might have more energy,' I snap. 'You're not even carrying anything.'

Why did he have to come with us?

We walk and walk. I keep an eye out for tree kangaroos but I only see things that slither and scuttle. Luckily nothing comes too close. Then suddenly Mawi halts, and somehow I stop myself from walking straight into her. Blake crashes into me.

165

'Watch it,' I say.

'Then don't just stop.'

'I had to.'

'*We* had to,' corrects Mawi. 'The ground's getting steeper. I need you both to be careful.'

Blake nods, but I scowl. I don't need to be told how to walk. I step past her and feel my mouth fall open. The land drops to our left, like a giant death slide, and the trees are too thick on our right to move over. Mawi has a point. We have to be careful.

With nowhere else to go, I tread along the narrow ledge, my feet at an angle. The others scuff the ground behind me. Then I hear a yell. Twisting round, I see Blake sliding down the steep slope on his back, barging through vines and roots. His arms flail out trying to grab something. At last he collapses at the bottom, and I burst out laughing. He swears loudly.

'Will one of you help me?' he shouts.

'I'll come and get you.' Mawi starts climbing down, cautiously finding tree roots for footholds.

'He can climb up himself,' I say.

'I can't. I'm stuck.'

'What do you mean you're—' Blake's feet and legs are lowering into bubbling mud. He's sinking. 'Quicksand!' I yelp.

Possibly not the best thing I could have done. Blake looks down and starts yelling and thrashing. He's going to be sucked in even faster.

'Keep your legs still.' I say, trying to calm him down. 'But see if you can reach a vine or root or something to pull yourself out.'

'I can't reach anything,' yells Blake, thrashing even more.

Mawi is still moving towards him, but she can't pull him out on her own.

'Stay still. I'm coming!'

I throw myself over the edge. My legs and back scrape against rocks and roots, I dig my heels into the earth, but I can't get a grip. I slide past Mawi, heading straight for Blake. I grab at something, anything, but I'm going too fast.

At this rate, I'll sink us both.

CHAPTER

29

My fingers close around a rock, stretching to keep a grip as gravity pulls me down. I slam my heels into the ground, and somehow manage to stop centimetres from the quicksand.

'Give me your hand,' yells Blake, waving his arms frantically, his legs completely submerged.

I'm about to stretch towards him, when I freeze, my mind flashing back to the sea. Mawi had been frantic and almost pulled me under. Blake is stronger. He'll drag me in. I search for a loose stick or vine on the hillside, but it's all been swept away.

'Mawi, we need a stick. Have you got one near you?' I shout up to her.

She scrapes the ground with her hands. 'I can't pull them out. I'll go back to the top and get one.' She scrambles up the slope.

I turn to Blake. 'You're going to be fine.'

'Get me out,' he yells, stretching towards me, his eyes wide.

'Listen, you need to stop moving. You're making yourself sink faster.'

His body stills. 'Help me,' he whispers.

'I will. I am.'

'I've got one,' yells Mawi.

A long stick rolls towards me and I grab hold of it. Grasping onto a tree vine for support, I lean forwards, thrusting the stick towards Blake. He takes it in both hands and I pull backwards.

'It's not working,' he yelps.

His bottom's almost under now.

'It will,' I hiss. 'Whatever you do, don't let go.'

I heave with all my might, a roar exploding from my mouth.

'I moved,' yelps Blake. 'Do it again.'

I keep on heaving, and his body jerks towards me. My shoulders, arms, back, and stomach burn, as I drag him out centimetre by centimetre. At last he slumps onto the steep hillside beside me, and clings onto the same vine. We lie against the earth. My body is in agony.

'Thanks,' says Blake.

'Don't mention it.' I point to the top. 'You ready?'

He nods, and slowly we clamber up the slope. Nothing like quicksand to keep you focused on not slipping back down again. We reach the top and Mawi flings her arms around Blake.

'I thought you were going to die,' she cries. Then leaps back. '*Urgh*, you stink.'

See—hugging Blake? Never a good idea!

We rest for a few minutes. Then with aching limbs, we walk again, all of us paying close attention to the land, looking out for dips or slides. We stop for water and snack breaks, none of us taking too much, when finally the trees start to thin. More importantly, the sun's beginning to set.

'Can you hear that?' says Mawi. 'Is it water?'

The waterfall—I saw it on the map.

With a spurt of energy, I dart through the trees. Then stop. We're standing at the edge of a horseshoe-shaped cliff. It's as if someone chiselled a deep semicircle out of the land, and covered it with the most exotic ferns and plants they could think of. Halfway across, water tumbles over steep stone, into a swirling pool of bright blue. Jagged rocks peep out of the river, and on the other side, the jungle begins again.

'It's beautiful. It's like paradise,' says Mawi.

For a moment we just inhale the view.

'How do we get past it?' says Blake, after a while.

'We don't. We go down,' I say.

'What do you mean—we go down?' He steps closer,

peering over the edge. 'We can't climb down, the rock's too steep.'

'I never said anything about climb.'

'Then how else do we—' He starts shaking his head.

'You can't be serious,' says Mawi.

'We have to jump into the river. There's a boat moored down there, on the other side. Alistair hid it for us. That's why we have waterproof bags.'

'I'd rather climb it,' says Mawi.

'Me too,' says Blake.

'With what? Do you have grappling hooks or a harness?'

'So we have to jump into the river?' demands Mawi, her eyes flashing. 'You knew about this! When were you going to tell us?'

'I showed you the map. Anyway, it's not that far down. Truck and Alistair have done it.'

'They're cyborgs, not real human beings,' says Blake.

'It's not as far as the last time we jumped,' I say to Mawi.

'I nearly drowned,' she says.

'It wasn't that bad.'

She stares into the water and gasps. 'It's just like it.'

'It's not that high.'

'I'm not talking about the height. I'm talking about the rocks and the small space for us to jump into.'

My eyes flicker over the jagged stones peeping out of the water. She's right. An uneasy thought creeps into my mind, but I push it away.

'There must be another way,' says Blake

'There isn't. Alistair would have told me if there was.'

We fall into silence, watching the water crashing down. It's no longer paradise, but a horror scene. But the longer we wait, the more anxious we'll get, the harder it will be.

'Think of your sisters and your dad,' I say.

'We're really doing this?' says Mawi, breathlessly.

I nod.

'Then we'd better hold hands, jump together,' she says.

'We can't. There's not enough space, one of us will hit the rocks. You two go together if you want.'

'No way,' says Mawi. 'I want to go with you.'

'What?' says Blake, his eyes darting between the pair of us, his face contorting into a mixture of surprise and anger.

Even I can't believe it. *She chose me!* I allow a small satisfied grin.

'But I want to go with Finn,' says Blake.

CHAPTER 30

Both stare at me expectantly.

'You've got to look after me. You've got to get me back to Dad, otherwise . . . ' Blake pulls a finger across his neck.

Yeah, I get it. I'm dead.

'But without me, this whole thing is pointless. You need me to get to the Ropen,' says Mawi.

I thought I wanted to be in demand. Now I'm not so sure.

'Why don't I go in first and wait for you down there? You two can jump in together. I promise I won't get out of the water. Then we'll all swim to safety.'

Mawi shakes her head. 'I'm not going in unless you

hold my hand.'

'Me neither,' says Blake.

I'll have to remind him about being so desperate to hold my hand when we get back to safety. *If* we get back.

I peer over the edge again. What if I jump now? They'll have to follow. But what if they don't? I'll have to find some way to get back up again.

'All right, we'll go in together,' I say.

'You said there wasn't enough room,' says Blake.

'We'll make it work. We have to.'

I put the rucksack on my shoulders and tie the loose straps around my middle. Mawi hoists the other one onto her back.

'No,' I say. 'If we're doing this, Blake's carrying it.'

'But—'

'He weighs more than you and I hate to say it, but he's probably stronger.'

She hands it over.

'It's heavy,' says Blake in surprise.

'Yeah—I think Mawi knows that!'

I wait until he's done up the straps. Then we stand at the edge of the cliff, our toes overhanging. I look down at the water crashing over the rocks. It's not *that* high, but there's hardly enough space for two people, let alone three. I need to aim us at the right spot. But what if one of them jumps too far? My heart starts pounding. They're looking at me for support, but what if I can't help them? What if they get hurt?

'You won't change your minds?' I say.

Both shake their heads, and their hands grip mine even tighter. I have to get us through this.

'All right then—on three.' I take a deep breath. 'One, two, three.'

We leap over the edge, their screams dissolving into the noise of pounding water. Hurtling through cold spray, we plunge into the river below. Deeper and deeper. My clothes and shoes drag me down, but so do Blake and Mawi. Panic rises in me. I'm not in control. I can't swim—they're holding me under.

I open my eyes—the water stings—and kick my legs. But we're still heading down. Blake releases his grip and he soars to the surface, his foot slamming into the side of my head. At least I have some control now. I pull at the water, and kick my legs. Then Mawi's hand slips from mine. I feel her grab for me, but I need to breathe. I claw for the surface, take a giant gulp of air, before diving back down towards her. Her arms are flailing wildly. I grab her by the waist and swim with one arm, propelling with my legs. As soon as we burst into the air, I hold her under the chin and tow her to the side of the river. This feels far too familiar.

Blake helps me drag her onto the bank. I lie on my back, the rucksack poking into me. I haven't got the strength to untie it. Mawi coughs and splutters beside me.

'We did it,' says Blake.

'It was harder than I thought,' I say.

Mawi rolls over until her face is centimetres from mine. I blink. I think she's going to kiss me. Thank me for rescuing her. My heart starts pounding more than it did when we were drowning.

'You said you wouldn't let go!' she shouts at me.

Oh!

'You left me down there!'

'I didn't leave you,' I yelp, scooting backwards. 'I went back for you. I couldn't breathe. I had to get to the top.'

'You let me go, and I can't swim.'

Surely I haven't heard her correctly. 'What do you mean you can't swim? You live on an island. You jumped in the sea when Novak asked you to.'

'I lied to Novak. I never learnt.'

'But your Dad takes you camping.'

'On land. We're not mermaids.'

'Why didn't you tell me?' I erupt.

I close my eyes and rest my head on the ground. Her fear makes perfect sense now.

Blake drops to his knees next to Mawi. 'Finn did help us,' he says.

Is he being nice about me?

Mawi starts crying, and Blake puts his arm around her protectively, as if I'm the bad guy.

You know—I am the one who got you both down here. I went back for her while you just . . .

'We need to find the boat,' I snap, jumping to my feet.

I fumble with the knot around my middle but finally manage to rip the bag off my back. Neither Blake nor Mawi move. In wet shoes I sludge along the edge of the bank, searching for the boat under ferns and massive plants I've no idea the names of. Looking over my shoulder, Blake's still got his arm around her. *Yeah, yeah, you sit there while I do all the work.* Insects swarm around me, attracted to wet hair and clothes. I twist around on my feet.

'You could help, you know!' I shout.

'In a minute. I'm just making sure she's all right,' calls Blake.

I snort. Should I sit down too? Leave it to them? Then in my mind I see Mum in the lounge with the doll, and I move even quicker.

CHAPTER

31

The sky is darkening, but it looks like it's going to be a full moon. I'll still be able to see. And the noises have changed. No birds now. But insects clicking, frogs croaking, and hisses from who knows what. At last I spot something sticking out from under some large green leaves. Yes!!!! A wooden rowing boat, with two oars. I hurry back to Mawi and Blake, who are still in the same position I left them.

'Found it,' I say flatly.

Scooping up my bag, I head back without waiting. I hear their footsteps and know they're following.

'Where's the engine?' says Blake, when we reach it.

'What, so we can let them know we're coming? We

need to make a stealth approach,' I say. 'Now are you going to help me or just watch while I pull it onto the river?'

'I'll help,' says Blake.

The boat's quite light and soon it's bobbing on half a metre of water. I clamber into the middle seat, dropping my bag into the foot well.

'You two sit either end, while I row. Then we can switch places,' I say.

Mawi sits opposite, while Blake climbs behind me. I pull the oars and start to row.

'Will there be creatures in there?' says Blake.

'Crocodiles,' Mawi and I say at the same time.

'Wish I hadn't asked.'

Then there is only silence, apart from the swishing of oars and creatures screeching in the trees. My arms begin to ache and sweat drips down my back and forehead. I wish we had an engine now. Who cares about the noise?

'I don't suppose either of you would like to take over?' I say.

'You're doing fine,' says Blake from behind me.

I roll my eyes. 'If we'd brought a sack of potatoes they'd have been more useful than you.'

'Yeah. At least we could have eaten them,' says Mawi, with a giggle.

I pause for a second. Did she just make a joke at Blake's expense? Then I burst out laughing. Blake remains silent.

'I'll do it, I'll row,' says Mawi.

'We'll have to move low in the boat, so it doesn't tip. Blake, you need to balance us out. If it looks like the boat is swaying one way, put your weight on the other side.'

I slip off my seat into the foot well and Mawi copies. Then we switch places. The boat wobbles, but is nowhere close to tipping. I'm about to tell Mawi what to do, when she grabs the oars and rows. She's faster than me.

'You've done this before?' I say, unable to keep the surprise out of my voice.

'Yeah. I row with Dad.'

'He lets you row when you can't swim?'

'We don't fall in,' says Mawi.

I shake my head in disbelief. Then pull out the map. Even in the full moon, I can't make out the markings or small writing, and so I search for my torch. Looking at the map again, I try to spot landmarks so I know where we are. I can't.

'How much further?' asks Mawi.

'Not too far,' I say, although I have no idea.

She gets us a good way up the river before she lays down the oars and rubs her biceps.

'Blake, it's your turn,' I say.

'I've never rowed before.'

'Then it's time you learnt.'

'But my contract . . . '

If we weren't at opposite ends of the boat, I'd punch him. I glower at him, then realize he's chuckling. 'Did you just make a joke?'

'Yeah,' he says chuckling even more. 'And if you're lucky, I might make another one.'

Whoa! He sounds almost human!

Mawi slinks into the foot well and Blake stands up. The boat lurches left and I throw myself to the right, trying to stabilize it.

'Keep low,' I shout.

He drops down, muttering, 'Sorry.'

Blake squeezes past Mawi and grabs the oars, while she falls into his seat. He stretches out his arms and lowers the base of the oars into the water. Then he pulls them back, and we don't move at all.

'You row the other way,' I say.

'I did that on purpose,' he says, and I can't work out if he's lying.

Blake rows for about five minutes. Sweat pours down his face, and he has to put the oars down at regular intervals.

'Meet Rio Dinoni, the all-action hero!' I say.

Blake puts on his smouldering smile, flashing his ready-for-Hollywood teeth. Then his mouth falls open. His hands shake and he drops an oar.

'What the . . .?' I gasp.

'Look behind you,' he hisses.

I turn to see two yellow eyes of a crocodile glinting in the moonlight.

CHAPTER

32

'I've lost an oar,' yelps Blake.

My eyes dart from the crocodile to the oar, now bobbing alongside the boat, next to me.

'You two need to lean the other way. I'm going to grab it,' I say.

'You can't put your hand in the water,' cries Mawi. 'Who knows how many crocs are down there?'

The oar begins to drift. It's now or never. Taking a deep breath, I lunge to my right. The others lean the opposite way, and I grasp the wooden pole, whisking my hand out of the river. Thank God, it's still attached.

'I'm not going to be the next Captain Hook,' I say.

'That was brilliant,' says Blake.

'Fantastic,' says Mawi. 'Now pass the oars back to me. I'll row.'

'You need to sit in the middle,' I say.

'I'm not chancing tipping the boat right now.'

'Good point. Blake, don't drop it,' I say, sliding the oar across.

He passes both back to Mawi and soon we're powering away.

'Do you think the croc's following us?' says Blake.

I shrug. Shining the torch on the water and the shore, I see dark shapes, but nothing comes too close. Soon the river becomes narrower, and we enter a ravine, steep rocks towering above us on either side, and I recognize where we are. It's on the map.

'Not too far now,' I say.

The rocky sides become less steep and at last I spot what I'm looking for. The cave. 'We need to pull over somewhere to my left. Over there,' I say, pointing the torch.

'Is that where the tribe is?' says Mawi, quietly. She sounds afraid.

'No. Alistair told me they have too many guards watching the river. We're going to sleep in the cave tonight and go to their village by land tomorrow.'

Mawi rows us towards a thin grassy strip, but we need to step into water before pulling the boat onto the shore.

'What if there are crocs about?' says Blake.

'We run fast.'

'I'm not sure I can outrun a crocodile,' he says.

'As long as I can outrun you, I'm fine.'

He frowns, as if he doesn't understand.

'They'll be busy eating you instead of me,' I add.

Scanning the land and water, I can't see any shadows, snouts, or eyes. Praying we're alone, I step into the shallows. My feet cause ripples but there doesn't seem to be any other movement in the river. I hold the boat and the others creep out. Grabbing our bags, we yank the boat onto the shore, then hurtle across the rocks and start to climb. Mawi's slower—but then she was rowing longer. At least Blake has the grace to carry her rucksack without moaning for once.

We climb higher and higher until we reach the entrance to the cave. I pause outside.

'What if something's in there?' says Mawi.

'Just what I was thinking. Let's send Blake in to find out. If he doesn't come out, the answer is yes.'

I feel two elbows in my ribs—one from each of them.

'I'm just trying to make him useful.'

Another two ribs in my sides, and we look at each other for a moment.

'Fine, I'll go in,' I say.

I step inside. I don't think crocs can climb but there could be snakes, spiders, and . . . does Papua New Guinea have bears? It's cooler in here, and damp. I shine the torch around the shallow cave and see a lump in the corner. My throat dries. Is it moving? Then I almost laugh out loud.

It's a pile of sleeping bags, pillows, and roll mats. Plus a coolbox, and a huge rucksack.

'It's safe,' I call to the others, grabbing the pack. I'm surprised it's not heavier.

Unzipping it, I suck in breath. Our mission feels even more real. It's filled with thick wire meshing, rope, and wooden stakes. I drop the bag, just as the others creep in. We rip open the coolbox to find bottled water, sandwiches, cake, and chocolate. There's enough for ten, let alone three.

'Alistair, I love you,' I whisper.

'I wouldn't go that far,' says Blake, stuffing a ham sandwich into his mouth.

We eat and eat, until Mawi slams the lid back onto the box.

'What are you doing?' I demand.

'We'll need some for breakfast. And you'll be sick if you eat too much.'

I lean back on the pile of sleeping bags and nod. She's right—of course.

'How many sleeping bags are there?' says Blake suddenly.

Sitting up, my heart sinks. 'Two.'

'I guess you two are sharing,' says Mawi.

'Never,' says Blake.

'I'd rather freeze.'

'Fine by me,' says Blake, grinning. 'I'll have the sleeping bag then.'

'I don't think so. You weren't supposed to be here. Alistair left it for me.'

His grin drops. 'We could light a fire.'

'And alert the villagers?' I close my eyes and then open them again. 'Got it. We should have a lookout. Someone can be outside while the other two sleep, and then we'll switch places.'

'It'll be cold outside at night,' says Mawi. Then she groans. 'We'll have to unzip one of the sleeping bags. The two inside will share it as a blanket, and the lookout can have the other one.'

I clamber to my feet. 'I'll be first lookout. Have either of you got an alarm?'

'I've got my watch,' says Blake.

'Set it for three hours. You two can work out who goes next.'

I grab a sleeping bag, leaving the roll mats and pillows for them. Then step back outside. I sink into the sleeping bag and lean against a mossy rock. The moon is like a giant silver balloon, illuminating the tops of cliffs and trees. I've never been abroad before and now this. I wish I could enjoy it. But tomorrow we're heading into a tribe who hate us. We're going to take away a Ropen that's their ally, if it's even there . . .

My mind whirs so much, I don't hear the footsteps.

'How are you?' says Mawi.

I almost leap out of my sleeping bag.

'Sorry, I didn't mean to startle you,' she says, putting

a roll mat down next to me and sitting on it.

'Has it been three hours?'

'Only one. I couldn't sleep.'

She shivers and I move onto the mat, unzipping my sleeping bag and spreading it over us to keep warm.

'I was going to relieve you. I'd be lookout so you could sleep,' she says.

'I'm not tired. Are you scared about tomorrow?'

'Terrified. Although I might finally find out why my great-grandfather was exiled.'

'Do you know anything about the village?'

'Not much. I know they believe everything has a soul, not just humans or animals. Every plant, stone, tree—and they care for them all, pray for them all. And if they take something from the forest, they replace it. Like if they eat a plant, they grow another.'

'Well that's good. They sound nice.'

'They told my great-grandfather that they would kill any member of his family if they ever stepped foot on Gamboi again. So I don't think they'll be that nice to me.'

I swallow hard. 'Know anything else about them?'

'I don't remember this. I was too young. But Mum told me Great-Grandfather used to carry out some of their customs. He'd invite everyone, and I mean everyone, in our neighbourhood to his birthday celebrations. He'd produce so much food, 'cause the more food you provide, the more guests you have—the wealthier and stronger you are. Apparently my great-grandmother used to get so mad because they weren't wealthy at all. Granddad tried to do it, but Grandma wasn't having any of it. My mum cooks amazing Gamboin food though. Her chicken dish is fantastic. I'm going to ask her for the recipe if we get back.'

'*When* we get back,' I say.

'You don't know what Novak wants me to do.'

I raise an eyebrow, waiting for her to continue.

'I've got to convince the tribe that my mum felt so bad about what Great-Grandfather did, that she's made an antidote for the venom.'

'How was she supposed to know their leader got sick?'

'She had a dream.'

'Oh!'

'Novak's great plan,' says Mawi flatly. She leans her head against the rock. 'It wasn't fear keeping me awake though. I couldn't sleep because of something else.'

'Is it because Blake snores? Please tell me he snores!'

'No,' she says with a laugh. Then her face falls serious. 'I didn't say thank you to you.'

'For what?'

'You saved my life in the water and I was so angry and mean.' She pauses. 'The thing is . . . I was angry with myself, not you. I'm really sorry.'

My body warms, and it's nothing to do with the sleeping bag. 'Well . . . you know what they say. You hurt the ones you love the most.'

She elbows me in the gut. 'I don't love you.'

'You sure about that?' I say with a laugh.

'Yes, I'm sure.'

'Sadly, I'm sure too. It's Blake you love.'

Even in the moonlight, I see her cheeks flush.

'That's not true.'

'It's not surprising really. Him being Blake Saunders. In fact I bet his armpits smell like roses.'

'Will you stop it?' she says, elbowing me again. 'Why do you hate him so much anyway?'

'I don't hate him.'

'But you don't like him.' I say nothing, so she continues. 'I don't blame you. Until this trip, he treated you like dirt.'

I look at her in surprise. I didn't think she'd noticed.

'I asked him why he did.'

My gut tightens. 'What did he say?'

'He said that something happened between the two of you, and you deserved everything you got.'

I lean back my head and close my eyes. 'He's not wrong.'

'So what happened?'

'He didn't tell you?'

'No.' She hesitates. 'Will you?'

Perhaps it's the moonlight. Perhaps I'm delirious from exhaustion. Or perhaps Mawi can ask me anything and I will answer. Because suddenly the words are tumbling out of my mouth.

CHAPTER 33

'Can you believe we were best mates for about a year?' I say. 'I won this scholarship his dad started. The Marcus Saunders Scholarship.'

'You won it?' says Mawi.

'You've heard of it?'

'Everyone who wants to be an actor's heard of it.'

'Well I won it in its first year. I started going to this drama after school and holiday club. It was on the other side of London from where I live, but it could have been a different world. Chauffeurs and nannies dropped off most of the kids. They lived in houses with more bathrooms than Mum and I had rooms, and they were so snobby. I wanted to quit; I hated it. But Mum was so proud of me. She wanted me to be an actor.'

'You didn't want to be one?'

I shake my head. 'Not at first, but then I got to know Blake. I think his dad forced him to be my friend. I wasn't like any of his other mates. Blake was Mr Popularity even when he was ten. But we started hanging out, and I'd go over to his house. He never came to mine though.' I fold my arms. 'Now I know it's because he wouldn't be seen dead in my part of London. His dad's all right, but his mum's a nightmare. She was the biggest snob of all. She hated it when I went round.'

'She's an actor too?'

'Yeah. She could have acted as if she liked me, but she used to make comments and look down her nose. Blake hated it.'

I lean back my head. I'd forgotten how much Blake used to stick up for me when his mum was mean.

'So Blake was nice to me, and we became really good friends. Best friends. I got popular too, and better at acting. We'd be paired together and he was amazing. Is amazing.' My mouth slams shut. I can't believe I said that.

'It sounds like you might be the one in love with him,' says Mawi, with a giggle.

I snort. 'He's amazing at acting. Nothing else. Surely you've noticed that!'

'His armpits smell of roses, too, remember?'

We both laugh. Then Mawi says softly, 'So . . . what happened?'

I take a deep breath. 'After about a year, there were auditions for this TV advert. It was the first role either of us were going to go for, and it was supposed to be this massive break. Whoever got it would be a star. We rehearsed together, and then one of us—I think it was Blake—said we'd fall out 'cause one of us would be jealous of the other. So we made a blood promise neither of us would go for it.'

'Blood promise?'

'We cut our fingers and wiped them together. You know—swapping blood.'

'That's disgusting.'

'We were eleven.' I smile as I remember Blake's face when I pricked his finger. He was a wuss even then. 'Anyway, I told my mum that I wasn't going for the audition and why, and she went mad. Ballistic. She kept going on and on about all the sacrifices she'd made for me. How we never had enough money and the hours she had to work. But I still said no. I'd promised Blake. But the day of the audition, Mum dragged me to the studio. She gave me such a guilt trip that I had to take a shot at it.'

'You got the part?'

'No, another kid did. Steve Griffin—have you heard of him? He's in lots of Disney programmes.'

Her eyes widen. 'Yes, I have.'

'I felt awful. I'd gone behind Blake's back.'

'But you had to because of your mum.'

'Blake wouldn't understand. His dad went mental

when he refused to go. But Blake told him that if he was made to go, he'd perform really badly to make sure he didn't get the part. And his mum didn't want him jeopardizing his career with a bad audition.'

'Jeopardize his career? He was eleven.'

'Welcome to the world of the Saunders.' I sigh. 'I never told Blake I went to the audition. I know it was stupid, but I thought he wouldn't find out because I didn't get the part. I forgot about his mum, who knows everyone and everything. She found out, and relished telling him. I think she even got hold of the tape and showed him my audition. By then, it was too late for me to tell him why. He wouldn't listen. He refused to speak to me, said I betrayed him, said I was a liar.' I turn to Mawi. 'You probably hate me now.'

She's silent for a moment. Yep, she hates me.

'Is that it?' she says, finally. 'I thought you were going to tell me something really interesting, like you'd killed his pet dog, or he'd killed yours, or something.'

'I broke a promise.'

'Everyone breaks promises. You had a good reason.'

'Did you not hear me say it was a blood promise?'

'I will never understand boys,' says Mawi. 'Did you still go to drama school together?'

'Blake's mum wanted me to lose my scholarship. But my mum went to see Mr Saunders, telling him all the pressure she'd put me under. He decided I could stay. It was pretty tough though. I had no friends. They didn't know exactly what happened, but they preferred Blake to me anyway. I was the outsider. Without Blake on my side, I was back to being the poor boy, charity case.' I pause. 'But then Blake left. He got role after role in various TV programmes, and then became Rio. He was too busy for drama school. He came back sometimes, but he'd really changed. He was so up himself. So like his mum. He treated people like dirt, and suddenly I didn't care that we used to be friends or what I'd done. I stood up to him. I wouldn't let him walk over anyone, and he hated that even more. We became absolute enemies.' I look at Mawi. 'Still think he's some great hero?'

Her eyes are closed and her breathing's heavy. I doubt she heard a word about him changing. I lean my head next to hers and drift off too.

CHAPTER

34

'Well isn't this cosy?'

My eyes open. Blake stands in front of me, smirking, the sun shining behind him. My brain tries to catch up—what am I doing here? Something shuffles to my left and my eyes dart in that direction. Mawi wakes with a snort, and suddenly I remember last night.

'Did your alarm not go off?' I say.

His smirk vanishes. 'I must have slept through it. But you're not exactly the best lookout are you?'

'You expected me to stay up all night?' I ask.

'Oh give it a rest,' says Mawi, climbing to her feet and stretching. 'Let's have some breakfast.'

We devour the rest of the coolbox. Stale cake has never tasted so good. Then Mawi disappears back into the cave to get ready.

'What's she doing in there?' I say. 'She's been ages.'

'She's a girl,' says Blake.

'We're going to a tribal village. She doesn't exactly have to—' I stop talking.

Blake's jaw drops. Mawi stands in the entrance to the cave.

'Don't say a word,' she orders.

She's wearing a simple red dress that shows off her beautiful brown skin. Her make-up is tribal—thick black liner causing her eyes to pop. White markings cover her cheekbones.

'This is what girls wear in the tribe. No jeans or shorts. I feel like I'm eight years old again.'

'You don't look eight! You look good,' I say.

'You look stunning,' adds Blake.

'Really?' She looks at Blake hopefully. 'I thought you were going to laugh at me for looking all girly.'

She doesn't look girly. She looks like a queen.

*

We shove the sleeping bags in the corner of the cave— they'll make a nice nest for an animal—and cover ourselves with insect repellent. It's hot and humid already, and I could do with deodorant, but Alistair didn't think to pack that. Or toothpaste. My teeth feel furry. I hand

Blake the massive rucksack, expecting him to complain, but he puts it on his shoulders without a word. Mawi and I take the other two. For the first time, I'm quite pleased Blake is with us, otherwise we'd be heaving luggage.

We follow the trail marked on the map, down from the rocks to a stretch of long razor-sharp grass. Luckily there's a well-trodden pathway.

'How much further?' says Blake, after a while.

'We can't be that far. We're on the tribe's footpath,' I say.

'What?' he yelps.

Mawi stops. 'No, we're not. I recognize this sort of track.'

'Then who made it?'

'Crocodiles. There must be nests around here.'

'What?' It's my turn to yelp. My eyes dart around nervously.

'If we leave them alone, they'll leave us alone. They'll be more concerned with their eggs,' she says.

'Or they'll be trying to protect them.'

Without another word, we speed up.

At last the long grass vanishes, and we hit the river again, just further up. Keeping an eye out for crocs and tribesmen, we creep along the bank, and after about a minute, we reach the wooden bridge, the last thing marked on the map. According to Alistair, the village is on the other side, encircled by mountains, obscured by jungle.

'There's no one here. There are no guards,' whispers Blake.

'None that we know of,' I say, before turning to Mawi. 'Are you ready?'

Suddenly she starts to shake, and her eyes widen like they did before she jumped over the waterfall. 'I can't do this,' she says.

'Yeah, you can. You'll be great.'

'No, I can't. We have to go back. We—'

Blake nudges me out of the way. He puts his hands on her shoulders. 'Mawi, you can do this. You will be amazing. You are strong, fierce. You have the blood of this tribe running through you. You speak their language. They're going to welcome you into their lives like we welcomed you into ours.'

Mawi gulps, but her eyes glisten.

'If you feel doubt—though you don't need to—dig deep. You are an amazing actor. I haven't worked with anyone as great as you before. You came in late and took everything on board. You can convince them to forgive you about your great-grandfather. You can fake your bravery.'

She starts to nod.

'Say after me—I can do this,' says Blake.

'I can do this,' she mutters.

'Louder.'

'I can do this,' she says.

'Yes, you can.'

He kisses her forehead and she closes her eyes. For a moment I think she's going to swoon. Then her eyes open, and she turns and steps onto the bridge.

Blake whispers, 'For all our sakes, I hope she can do this.'

'What? But you believe in her. You just said—'

'I was acting. It's what I do.'

For once, I'm grateful that he really is that good.

Mawi gets halfway across when I hear a grating sound, like an old clock being wound. Then the floor of the bridge splits in two, bascules rising like wings.

'They're lifting the bridge,' I gasp.

A deep voice yells something and an arrow flies through the air. Mawi spins around, and sprints towards us.

'Get out of here,' she shouts.

She slides down the rising bascule and lands at the bottom. Blake grabs her hand and pulls her up.

They start to run when I shout, 'Stop.'

CHAPTER

35

'Stay here, and wait for my call,' I shout, before running onto the inclining bridge.

My feet are already at 45 degrees. I pump my arms and legs as hard as I can. I think I can make it, but I don't have long. If the bridge lifts too high, there's no way I'll be able to jump to the other side. I'll fall into the river with the crocs.

Adrenalin surging, I grab the top of the bascule and scramble onto the ledge. My hands grip the rim, my legs bent, my feet balancing, just like I did on Tower Bridge. The gap between the two segments is widening more and more. I leap forward like a frog. My fingers grasp hold of the other bascule, and my body swings through the air. The bridge still rises, but at least I'm on the right side. With screaming biceps, I pull myself over the top. Arrows fly towards me. A man laces another arrow in his bow. I hurtle down the raised bridge, aiming straight for him. An arrow shoots past, so close the air whips me.

Charging for him, I bend low and kick my leg, hooking the bow with my toes. It yanks out of the man's grasp and skids across the ground. Suddenly I see the sharp point of a stone dagger. He thrusts it towards my chest. I spin and kick, this time my foot slams into him and he falls backwards. I'll kick again if I have to, but his chest is the only part of his body that's moving. I prod him gently with my shoe. No reaction. I think he's out cold, but who knows for how long?

I turn to the bridge, instantly spotting the large wooden wheel. I grab hold of it, and twist. The bascules begin to lower again, and at last I see Mawi and Blake on the other side.

'Run now,' I yell. 'The gap's not that far.'

Holding hands, they race across the bridge and jump over the narrow gap of the river, until they're stood beside me.

'What did you do?' says Mawi, staring at the man.

'Karate,' I say.

Both look at me with a mixture of horror and admiration.

'Is he dead?' says Blake.

'No! What do you think I am?' Then I look around

nervously. 'I thought there'd be more than one guard, and someone might have heard.'

We stay still and silent, but thankfully no one comes.

There's a thick wall of trees and foliage, running parallel with the river. According to Alistair, this is as far as his team came before the tribe ambushed them.

'Is there an entrance?' says Mawi.

'There must be.'

We creep along the jungle hedge, looking for a door or gate, all the while watching out for arrows. Then at last we come to a short narrow archway.

Mawi sucks in breath. 'I guess it's my turn now.'

'We know you can do it,' says Blake.

She bends down to go through the archway when I grab her shoulder. 'Halfway through, you should announce your arrival. Shout something. That guard at the bridge didn't give you a chance to speak.'

Mawi nods, and slips under the arch. We follow, stopping when she does. She shouts something, I have no idea what, and suddenly there are footsteps. Lots of them.

'I can do this,' whispers Mawi under her breath, before stepping out.

I nod at Blake and we walk through at the same time.

Mouths drop and spears thrust towards us. A group of seven men and three women make a semicircle, their eyes almost popping out of their heads. My expression must mirror theirs. They look like tribal warriors; men wearing loincloths, and straps around their chests with stone daggers fitted inside; lumpy scars like reptile skin covering their bodies. The women are covered with the same scars, but wear grass skirts and woven tops.

Mawi starts talking again. The warriors glare, when a boy appears, wearing denim shorts and a t-shirt. The men and women draw apart, allowing him through. The boy speaks, and Mawi gasps.

'He's their leader,' she whispers.

Seriously? He's my age!

While he talks, Mawi translates out of the corner of her mouth. 'His father is the true leader of the Gamboi tribe, but he's dying. Swando—that's the boy's name—has taken over his role.'

My stomach jolts. Novak's been spreading death everywhere. Conner and the cameraman with gas. Swando's father with adder poison.

'I'm going to tell him why we're here,' says Mawi. She bites her bottom lip. 'I'll have to tell him my great-grandfather's name.'

'You've got this,' I say, trying to sound as convincing as Blake.

She looks at me hopefully, then turns, and speaks in a solemn voice. If I didn't know her, I wouldn't have thought she was scared. I watch Swando carefully, but can't read his expression. Then Mawi says two words I recognize. 'Kins Oxlade'.

At once the warriors snarl and thrust their spears towards her. Swando spits words. For a second I think he might attack. Although our odds are very bad—eleven against us—I tense, ready to fight.

'He says we're foolish to come here,' whispers Mawi.

Too right!

'He says he should kill us. If he was his father, we'd be dead already.'

'Let's get out of here,' hisses Blake, pulling her arm.

But Mawi doesn't step back. Instead she stands taller and speaks louder, more commanding. Then she bends down and pulls a first aid box from her bag. I'm guessing it's the antidote.

Swando and Mawi talk, back and forth. It sounds like an argument. I glance at Blake who shrugs. Finally Mawi says in English, 'He's thinking about it.'

Swando points at Blake and me.

'He's asking why white boys are here,' Mawi translates.

'Tell him we volunteered,' I say. 'Tell him we wanted to help you cross the island, as you had to land on the other side.'

They talk some more, and with narrowing eyes, Swando steps closer to me.

'He's impressed white boys managed to cross the land. He's also surprised you knocked out his trained guard.'

'You told him that?'

'He asked me how we got past.'

Swando steps even closer, and I fight the urge to step back.

'You be lucky,' says Swando, his breath on my face. 'Normally more warriors at river, but they guard my father because he sick.'

'You speak English!' I exclaim.

'My father taught me,' he says. 'He and me the only ones that do. We travel to Port Moresby buy and sell goods for our village.'

'Why didn't you speak English earlier?' I blurt.

'I listen your conversation,' he says, with a smirk. Then he sidesteps in front of Blake. 'You Rio. I see you on bus in Port Moresby.'

No way??? We're in the deepest rainforest and Blake gets recognized.

'I'm Blake Saunders, the actor of Rio.'

Swando closes his eyes for what seems like forever. The warriors snarl.

At last he opens his eyes, and exhales loudly. 'I think I have nothing lose. My father very sick. We tried everything else. I take you to our village, but if he no recover—it is you who pay.'

CHAPTER 36

There might be spears at our backs, but for a moment, I forget to be scared. I don't think I've ever seen anything so cool in my life. Wooden houses are high up in the trees, lining a clearing, like houses back in England surround a park. Some are taller than others and I wonder if they've got more than one floor. Ladders spiral from the ground, around tree trunks until they reach the doorways. There are huts on the ground too, with chickens running in and out of one of them. Goats in another. The older people and warriors wear loincloths or grass skirts and tops. Girls wear dresses and the boys wear shorts and t-shirts. Little children are naked. They all stop and stare, whisper and point. Then I remember to be scared.

People snake down ladders towards us, but no one gets too close. Swando starts talking and the entire village gazes at us. I feel like a weird creature in a zoo. I'm not sure many of them have ever seen a white boy before. We follow Swando through the silent, parting crowds, until we reach a large hut. He opens the wicker door and I hear chanting.

'That's their doctor,' explains Mawi. 'He's with Swando's father.'

She steps into the hut, and I automatically follow when something sharp jabs my neck. I freeze, my eyes darting to Swando who's holding a spear to my throat.

Mawi spins round. 'No one's allowed in here but the doctor, Swando, his mum, and now me.'

'You can't go in there on your own,' I whisper.

'I have to. I'll be all right.'

I tense as the door closes behind her. Swando lowers his weapon, but doesn't move, and he glowers at me warningly. Blake and I stand beside the hut, and I shuffle uncomfortably under everyone's gaze. Blake doesn't seem affected. He must be used to this. He puts on his best smouldering smile, and I'm sure I hear girls gasp.

I glance back at the door. What's taking so long? Swando must be thinking the same. He barges past me, and slips inside.

The villagers get bored looking at us. Some return to their houses, others feed the animals or whittle spears out of wood. The younger children play football or a game that looks like bowling with stones. There's a sense of calmness, contentment, and peace amongst everyone.

A group of girls hover nearby, wearing dresses and make-up similar to Mawi. Blake winks at them and they collapse into giggles. I wink too, and they giggle again.

'Wow Finn, I think you might finally have found some fans,' whispers Blake.

The door opens and Mawi walks through, her eyes worried.

'You okay?' I whisper.

'He's really sick,' she says. 'Swanso's mum refuses to leave his side.'

Suddenly the entire village falls silent, the animals too. I turn around. A man stands in the doorway wearing an enormous feathered headdress and markings cover his face. Is that the doctor?

He barks an order and we're surrounded with spears again. Oh God—has the leader died? Did the injection kill him? I glance at Mawi, but she's staring straight ahead.

The warriors thrust their weapons in our direction, making us move. Clutching our rucksacks, we're herded through the village to a part where there are no houses in the trees, just old and decrepit huts on the ground. Vines hang like bunting between the roofs, but instead of flags, skulls dangle down. I want to throw up but I mustn't show fear.

We stop beside a tree that has an old ladder wrapped

around its trunk. I crane my neck to see a house miles above. At least that's what it looks like.

'We have to climb,' whispers Mawi, grabbing a rung.

I follow her, trying to ignore the splintered, thinning wood. The ladder pulls tight, and I glance down to see Blake and two warriors climbing it too. Can the ladder take all our weight? With sweaty palms, I go round and around the trunk. Higher and higher. *Just don't break!* At last I reach the front door and practically throw myself inside after Mawi. The room is completely bare. Wooden walls, wooden ceiling—that's it. As soon as Blake's inside too, the door slams, leaving the warriors on the outside. Dim light steals through gaps in the thatched roof.

I hear the scraping of wood. 'Are they locking us in?'

Mawi nods. 'They'll let us out when their leader is better.'

'How long will that take?'

'I've no idea,' she says.

My body grows cold. 'We only have one day left, before . . . the dolls . . . '

'You think I don't know that?' she snaps.

Blake's face whitens. 'We're their prisoners? What if their leader never gets better?'

And where's the Ropen? I haven't seen a single sign of it.

CHAPTER
37

Just when I thought it couldn't get any worse, rain hammers on the roof. It pours through gaps in the thatch, and we huddle in a corner trying to stay dry. Lightning illuminates the room. If it strikes this house, we're done for. A huge crack of thunder erupts ... followed by a deafening screech, a mixture between a roar and a squawk. I've never heard anything like it.

'The Ropen?' whispers Mawi.

'I think so.'

'She sounds terrified.'

'Not the only one,' says Blake.

'At least we know she's here,' I say.

Every time there's thunder, we hear another panicked

screech. Part of me wishes I could see the creature, calm her down. The other part—the bigger part—wants nothing to do with her. Do Ropens eat humans?

We spend the next half hour going over and over Alistair's plans on how to catch her. So many things could go wrong, but I can't think like that!

'You do realize Novak had this all planned out,' says Mawi. 'Our stunts were to prepare us for this. To get us here to—' Her words drip away.

'Yeah, I realized,' I say. 'Novak's obsessed and . . .' My words drip away too.

Time drags, and time is the one thing we don't have. How long before the dolls are activated? The rain keeps pouring, and puddles spread on the floor. The light through the gaps in the roof begins to fade.

'They're going to let us starve in here,' says Blake. 'Then they'll hang our skulls on the bunting outside.'

'Do you know why they do that?' I say to Mawi.

She nods. 'It's a way to remember the dead. They pray under their skulls to honour them.'

We fall into silence.

I must doze off because I jolt awake when the door opens. It's dark and the rain has stopped. A warrior slams the floor with her spear and I half expect the house to crack. She bows, then speaks.

'We're invited to dinner,' says Mawi.

'At least they're not letting us starve,' I say.

We're led back through the village, and I can hardly

believe my eyes. I thought the village was cool in the daytime, but at night it's spectacular. Neon blue light shines out of woven wooden spheres dangling from the trees. They light up the houses, the clearing. But there can't be electricity here. How can these work? I want to take a closer look, but we're kept on the path.

We're taken to the top floor of a tree house built on two levels. We sit on either side of a carved wooden table with a line of warriors standing behind. Swando sits at the head of the table, a wooden ball of blue light hanging above him. And I realize I've seen this light before—shining out of Truck's bag the night Anna and I were in the pool.

Swando puts his hands together as if praying. 'My father drink water now. He sit up in bed. I feed you as way of thanking. And father say—we forgive family of Kins Oxlade.'

'You do?' says Mawi,

'Forgive but no forget.'

'That's great.'

She looks so happy; I think *she's* forgotten the real reason we're here. The Gamboins aren't going to forgive us for capturing the Ropen.

'Why was my great-grandfather asked to leave?'

Swando's eyebrows rise. 'You not know?'

'No one would tell me.'

'I tell you. But first we eat celebration feast.'

'Celebration feast?' she yelps, then forces a smile onto her face.

What's wrong with a feast? I thought we were hungry.

A line of girls and boys, about our age, come in and out of the room, setting covered wooden bowls on the table.

'Wouldn't it be easier if we ate downstairs? They have to carry everything up the tree,' I say.

'They used to it,' says Swando.

I shuffle uncomfortably. It seems wrong that they're waiting on us. Blake on the other hand looks the most comfortable I've seen him on this island. Soon the table is full, and Swando claps his hands. The warriors step forward and take the lids off the bowls.

Oh! Now I know what's wrong with a feast.

Vegetables and dumplings are in one dish, but the others are bursting with thick maggots or spindly bugs.

'Gamboin delicacies.' says Swando. 'Sago grubs, stick insects.'

I glance at the others. Blake's turning green, and Mawi leans towards me whispering, 'Mum never made me eat these.'

Come on guys—we're supposed to be actors.

Blake clutches his stomach and suddenly looks so sad and pitiful. 'I would love to try some, but I'm just not hungry. I think it's the heat.'

Swando's eyes narrow, and I have a horrid feeling Blake's been incredibly insulting.

'It looks great,' I lie.

Swando nods. Using his fingers, he picks up a thick brown grub. 'Been roasted over fire,' he explains.

He hands the bowl to Mawi, who hesitates for a second before taking one. If she can do it, so can I. We look at each other, then shove the grubs into our mouths. Actually, it doesn't taste too bad—a bit like bacon.

'That was great,' says Mawi. Then she leans back and clutches her stomach too.

Don't you dare!

'But I think I'm a bit like Blake. I can't eat anything else. I'm really full.'

I could kill them both.

'You full too?' demands Swando.

'Yes,' is on the tip of my tongue, but I remember how hurt Mum was when Novak refused a biscuit, and these are Gamboin delicacies. I shake my head.

'Good.' Swando reaches for a bowl packed with plump white grubs, about four centimetres long. 'These not cooked. You don't eat the head,' he says, choosing one.

'You eat them raw?'

'For celebration feast. Very good for you.'

He bites the grub in two, and drops the head into an empty bowl. I glare at Blake and Mawi, both looking as if they're trying to decide whether to laugh or vomit. I take a deep breath and grab a grub. Oh God—it feels squidgy. But if I'm going to do this, I'll have to be quick. I tear off the body with my teeth, and chomp down. It explodes in my mouth, and I force myself to swallow.

'Delicious,' I croak.

Swando smiles before lifting up a bowl of stick insects.

Somehow I manage to eat something from every dish . . . and really, it all tastes fine. It's only the thought of it that puts me off. Swando beams and claps me on the back, and I can't help but grin. We're gaining trust.

Suddenly there's a screech. I stiffen. We can't show too much excitement or interest.

'What's that?' says Blake casually, as if it was just a dog barking.

'Come. I show you something,' says Swando.

CHAPTER 38

I follow Swando into the clearing, and forget about my churning stomach. My heart thuds in my ribcage. Beside me, Mawi and Blake gasp. Novak was right. The Ropen lives. A glossy black pterodactyl, the size of an elephant, stands in the centre. Bat-like wings tuck in to her sides. Jagged teeth run along the edge of her long pointed black beak. Bright yellow eyes gaze at us. But it's the neon blue covering her underbelly all the way to the tip of her tail that takes my breath away.

'Wow!' says Blake.

'She's beautiful,' I whisper.

Mawi takes one step closer. 'She's amazing.'

'She is,' says Swando.

'The blue in the balls around your village—that's from her isn't it?' I ask.

'Droplets fall from tail. She let us have them. The blue not only bring light, but give protection from crocodile.'

'How?'

'Crocodile hate smell. They keep away from village. We, in return, protect her egg from giant rat.'

'Giant what?' My eyes dart over the ground.

'Rat. Nasty things. Also we give Ropen a delicacy.'

'Worms?'

Swando laughs. 'Not my delicacy. Hers. Goat.'

Why couldn't I have had goat?

'Every fifty year she lay one egg. Sometimes they no make it because of rat. So for hundreds and hundreds of years, Gamboins help.'

'Every fifty years?' exclaims Mawi. 'How old is she?'

'We not know. But last time she lay egg, a Gamboin stole it. That's why he were made to leave.'

I tear my eyes away from the Ropen. Mawi's jaw drops. Blake curses under his breath.

'My great-grandfather?' she whispers.

'Kins Oxlade planned sell it in Port Moresby. He was one of elders who visited big island.'

Mawi clasps her hands to her mouth. 'I'm so sorry.'

'Luckily my great-grandfather catched him and sent him to Port Moresby, telling him never to return.'

Mawi twists around to face Blake and me. 'So my family did know about the Ropen? They never said.'

More importantly, someone must have told Novak!

The Ropen stamps her claw, her talons scraping through the leaves and mud.

'She get impatient.' Swando looks at me pointedly. 'You, come.'

The other two remain where they are, while I follow Swando towards the beautiful black creature. Swando puts his hands on her neck, and she lays her beak on his head, closing her bright yellow eyes. Close up, I see small reptilian scales covering her wings and body.

'They're the markings on your skin,' I say to Swando.

'Yes. At thirteen, if you pass warrior test, you have markings of Ropen inked into you.'

'Ouch!'

Swando grins. 'Does hurt. You want touch her?'

'Can I?'

'Yes. You have warrior spirit in you. Girl have warrior spirit in her too, but she family of Kins Oxlade.'

He doesn't mention Blake, and I feel ridiculously pleased.

Reaching out my arm, I lay my hand against her neck. She stiffens for a second, then turns her head and rests her beak on my hair. I could stay like this forever.

'She trust warriors,' says Swando. 'But now you step back. It is time for treat.'

'Treat?'

I step back, and see a man leading two goats into the clearing. Ah! The man takes the lead off one goat only.

'The second goat for her mate,' explains Swando. 'She take it to him after she eaten.'

'There are two Ropens?' I exclaim.

Nodding, Swando says, 'Male sit on egg right now. We have warriors guarding nest.'

He pulls a wooden whistle out from the belt across his chest. The Ropen sets her yellow eyes on him, and claws the ground. Swando blows the whistle. I don't hear a thing, but the Ropen spreads her wings out. It must be like a dog whistle, too high-pitched for human ears.

'She come whenever I use this,' says Swando.

The Ropen soars into the air, encircling us. Against the black night, she's a huge neon strip streaking round and round. She dives to the ground and grasps the goat in her beak. She shakes her head, whipping it from side to side, like a dog with a squirrel. I can't tear my eyes away from her. It's disgusting, scary, but . . . amazing all at the same time.

The bones crunch as she rips it apart.

Then there's a thud.

'Blake's fainted,' says Mawi.

✳

Half an hour later, we're in a room covered with furs, in a bedroom in Swando's tree house. There's no doubt about it. As comfy as it is, many, many tree kangaroos died for this bedding. We lie on top, since it would be scorching to use them as covers.

'This my father and mother's room. They no been here since he were ill.'

'We can't sleep here then,' says Mawi. 'It's their's.'

'My mother wish you have best night sleep. I be next door. Then tomorrow we have big celebration with dance and music for father getting better and for you, our honoured guests. I might even wear loincloth,' he adds, with a smile.

'Why don't you?' I ask. 'Why do you wear shorts and t-shirt?'

'Warriors, parents, and grandparents like traditional dress.' Then his smile grows even wider. 'Do you like wearing same clothes as your parents?'

'Absolutely not,' I say, grinning back.

But as he closes the door, my grin drops. I feel sick. It's nothing to do with the grubs I ate or the Ropen demolishing a goat. Swando has to be one of the coolest people I've ever met and I'm going to steal from him. I have to . . . for Mum. I think the others feel the same because no one speaks. We lie in silence, listening to the screeching, chirping, and squawking of whatever creatures are out there.

My alarm is set for 1 a.m. Part of me hopes it won't go off.

CHAPTER

39

Even though the beeps are low, my alarm sounds deafening to me. I bolt upright, slamming the button on my watch. Swando *can't* wake up. I nudge Blake.

'Huh?' He snorts, rubbing drool off his chin. I wish his fans could see him now.

'It's time,' I whisper.

His eyes flash open.

'You wake Mawi, then go down the ladder. Get the net ready. Mawi knows what to do.'

'You're not coming?' he whispers.

'I will, but slight change of plan. I'm going to get Swando's whistle first.'

Blake nods.

'Don't forget the bags,' I say.

Grabbing my rucksack, I ease open the door to Swando's room. It's much smaller than the one we were in. Swando is sprawled out over furs, sleeping soundly. This feels so wrong. The ladder creaks outside. That must be Mawi and Blake. I hope for all our sakes there are no warriors in the clearing.

My eyes grow accustomed to the darkness, and I scan the room for the belt. Where is it? Then my stomach drops. I don't believe it—it's still tied around Swando's chest. As quietly as I can, I creep over the furs. Thank God they muffle my footsteps. My heart pounds so loudly though, I'm surprised it's not waking him up.

Hardly daring to breathe, I crouch down beside him. I reach for his torso, when he twitches. I freeze.

He rolls over.

Sweat trickles down my back as I lean over him. My fingers grasp the wooden whistle and I tug.

It's stuck.

I'm going to have to do this fast, like pulling a plaster off a leg. I yank the whistle as hard as I can and it jolts out of its sheath. I stumble backwards, my arms flail, desperately reaching for something that isn't there. Somehow I stop myself from landing on my bum. And somehow Swando doesn't wake up.

As fast as I can, I creep out of the room and slink down the ladder. Luckily there are no warriors. I hurry over to the goat hut and find a rope dangling from a hook. Making a quick slipknot, like a lasso, I turn to face the goats. *Oh no.* Which one do I choose?

Stomach twisting, I shove the loop over the nearest goat's head and tug it outside. It follows happily, bending its head every so often to grab a mouthful of mulch. I lead it through the village, past the skull bunting, past the decrepit tree house until we're hidden in the jungle. There's no sign of any blue light. Can crocs come to this part?

Shaking that thought away, I join the others. Blake's fiddling with a net stretched out beneath a palm tree. Mawi is putting the wooden stakes in place, just like she did when we caught the pig.

'Lucky there was so much rain. The ground's soft,' whispers Mawi, spotting me.

'Did you get it?' says Blake.

I hold the whistle in the air. 'Couldn't you have found a smaller palm tree?' I say. 'I can't reach the top to pull it down. I'm going to have to climb it.'

'It's got to be bigger than the Ropen,' says Mawi.

Of course!

'It should bend though. It's not that old,' she adds, throwing me the roll of wire.

I pass the goat to Blake. Then with my arms and feet wrapped around the bark, I scale the palm, letting the wire unravel at the same time. The tree buckles. Oh God—don't snap. Luckily it takes my weight. As soon as I reach the top, I wrap the wire round and round the trunk. It's not *that* high, so I jump to the ground, pulling the wire tight. The tree bends with me. *Yes!*

I hand the wire to Mawi. While she connects it to the top wooden stake, I take the goat from Blake.

'Sorry about this,' I whisper, leading it into the centre of the net.

The goat just looks at me. I tiptoe away but the goat follows.

'What are you doing?' I hiss. 'Go back.'

It stands there, chewing.

'You do know it's a goat? It doesn't understand you,' says Blake.

I lead it into the middle again, and walk backwards holding my hand out flat. The stupid goat follows.

'Tranquillize it,' says Mawi. 'Give it some pellets meant for the Ropen. With the size difference, they should knock it out.'

Grabbing some pellets, I stand in the middle. The goat gobbles them down. Novak said the effects were immediate, but who knows for sure? And the sky's lightening. To my utter relief, less than a minute later, the goat sways, and its legs buckle.

'If you're asleep when the Ropen comes, it'll be easier for you,' I whisper, stroking the goat's ears.

Then I shower the animal with pellets, hoping the Ropen will at least swallow some of them. Hurrying off the net, I watch Mawi expertly knot the wire and rope together. She nods and I blow the whistle. Like last time, I hear nothing.

'Blow it again,' says Blake.

I do as he says, and all of a sudden there's the beating of wings. I turn to see a neon flash above me.

The Ropen pounces on the net, biting the goat around the neck. The wire tightens, the stake topples, and the four corners of the net snap around her. It doesn't swing into the air but rolls across the ground as the Ropen thrashes her body. Her beak opens and the sleeping goat drops out. If she keeps thrashing, she'll squash it. That seems even worse than eating it. To my horror, she starts screeching. I don't think any pellets got inside her.

Quickly, I crouch down, poking my fingers through the net. She quietens and stills, my touch calming her.

I look over my shoulder. 'You two, go to the top of the cliff and light the flares.'

'Aren't you coming?' says Mawi.

'I will when the helicopters arrive. I don't want to leave her alone. Not like this.'

'The flares will wake the tribe,' says Mawi.

'If they come, I'll run.'

Blake tugs her arm. 'He'll have a better chance without us.'

They charge deeper into the jungle, heading for the cliffs.

'It's okay, it's okay,' I say soothingly to the Ropen.

She looks at me with such hope, as if expecting me

to let her out. For the next few minutes, I stroke the side of her neck, my eyes growing wet. If only there were another way.

BANG!

Red light explodes across the sky.

I jump, dropping the whistle. The Ropen screeches, and I hear cries from the village. The Ropen throws herself against the net again. I leap out of the way as she rolls across the floor. Somehow the goat's on top of her rather than underneath.

Helicopters roar over the tops of the trees, and grabbing my rucksack, I run.

War cries get louder. I glance over my shoulder and my blood turns to ice. Warriors with arrows and spears charge straight for me, Swando at the front.

CHAPTER

40

Vines, branches, sharp leaves scratch my clothes, my skin, but I don't stop. The warriors' footsteps and war cries grow louder. Arrows whizz past and a stitch slices through my stomach. Reaching the cliff, I crane my neck upwards. The white stone is almost vertical, but if Mawi and Blake can make it, so can I.

Shoving my toes in footholds, I seize handholds and storm up the side of the cliff. Glancing down, I swear under my breath. Warriors are climbing the wall as if they're running on flat ground. Ignoring my burning thighs, I climb higher and higher. At last I reach the top and fling myself over.

And there is the helicopter; its rotor blades spinning.

Truck jumps out, leaving Mawi and Blake peeping through the open door. Their mouths open and I know they're shouting but I hear nothing over the whirring of the helicopter. Then arrows whizz past. Without looking back, I know the warriors are over the top. Heart gurgling in my throat, legs about to collapse, but I keep going. Grit flies in the wind of the helicopter straight for my eyes. Squinting, I run even faster. Now only steps away, a spear flies past.

I turn to see Swando closing the gap between us, anger oozing from every pore.

'I'm sorry,' I shout, knowing he can't hear.

Truck grabs hold of me, flinging me inside. I slide across the floor and he jumps in after. The helicopter rises. Blake pulls the door shut, as arrows bounce off the side of the aircraft.

'Did they get the Ropen?' I ask.

'They lifted her,' says Blake.

Peering out, I see the warriors, but I also notice a small bundle of brown fur bounding near them on the ground. A tree kangaroo. Maybe they do bring luck after all.

The journey passes in a blur. Alistair's flying but I can't bring myself to talk to him or Truck. When we arrive at the hotel, Mawi, Blake, and I head straight to our rooms. I collapse on my bed and fall fast asleep.

*

The following morning, my eyes open blearily. My brain's fuzzy. I can't work out where I am.

'Good morning,' says a woman with an Eastern European accent.

I bolt upright. Novak's sitting on a chair beside the end of my bed. Suddenly everything comes back to me.

'The dolls,' I say. 'Have you disabled them?'

'Your mama is fine.'

'I want to see for sure,' I say, jumping to my feet. I'm still wearing the clothes from last night but I don't care.

'I really think you should lie back down.'

'I really don't care what you think,' I say, shoving on trainers, hurrying across the room.

'I see you're still cross with me.'

'You think?' I twist around to look at her. 'You need to show me my mum is okay right now or I'm going to call the police.'

'I do not like being threatened Finn, but . . . Mawi and Blake have been telling me how great you were in the—'

'Are they okay?' I interrupt.

Her lips purse. 'They are fine, as are their families.' Then she stands. 'I see we are not going to get anywhere until you know your mama is safe. So let's go.'

The hotel is a lot busier than the last time I was here; so many film crew milling about, all looking at me with a mixture of horror and awe. I wonder what they've heard.

'How's the Ropen?' I say, walking through the lobby.

229

'Still asleep.'

'She ate the tranquillizers then?'

'No. One of my men shot her from the helicopter. She was getting too stressed.'

I close my eyes, wishing I hadn't asked.

'One day, Finn, you will thank me for all you achieved. I got you to push yourself.'

My eyes flash open. 'I achieved them because I thought I was going to die.'

'Yes, death is a great motivator.' She looks at me expectantly. Does she want gratitude?

Suddenly a screech cries out making my blood curdle. Novak clasps her hands to her face.

'She's awake. Shall we see her?'

I really want to, but I say, 'I need to know Mum's safe first.'

'We can do both at the same time.'

'How? Unless the Ropen's in the glass room.'

We head into the gardens, but instead of going to the warehouse around the back, Novak leads me to the clearing where the mechanical Ropen was. There's a thick crowd of people around the cage, and the whole area is filled with cameras, tripods, and cranes, no one manning them yet. Out the corner of my eye, I see a goat tethered to a tree, munching on grass. *You survived!*

The screeching gets louder, more frantic.

'You put her in there?' I say, running towards the cage, squeezing past film crew, Novak right behind me.

The Ropen's on her feet, trying to spread her wings, but they're crushed up against the railings with only black scales squeezing out. Her yellow eyes are wide, filled with panic; her head almost touches the ceiling.

'You can't keep her like this,' I say.

Novak's smile drops, and she glances between the film crew and me. She leans in and whispers, 'Finn, never tell me what I can or cannot do. Anyway, I thought you were more concerned about your mama.' The menace in her words unmistakable. I gulp, my anger making room for fear.

Novak smiles again. She stretches her arms out wide, and cries, 'Isn't she the most magnificent creature you have ever seen?'

The crowd cheers.

'She's beautiful.'

I stare at the man who spoke. The world seems to tilt. I grab onto the metal cage to stop myself from falling.

CHAPTER

41

The screeching doesn't stop, but seems to fade into the background. My heart pounds in my ears.

'Conner!' I gasp. 'And . . .' Oh—I never found out the cameraman's name.

'No way!' says Blake, hurtling into the clearing, followed by Mawi.

Their eyes dart from the Ropen to Conner to me. Suddenly Mawi's by my side, her hand slipping into mine. She's trembling. I try to squeeze her hand, but realize I'm shaking just as much.

'Everyone but the children—LEAVE,' barks Novak.

The crowd melts way, leaving six of us. Two sets of three, facing each other.

'You're alive,' I whisper, my eyes locked on Conner's. 'The gas didn't kill you.'

'Why children, there was never any gas in the dolls to begin with,' says Novak. 'It was all an illusion, and no CGI needed.' The pounding in my ears gets louder. 'You should all be pleased. Your parents, your sisters, Anna—none of them were ever in harm's way.'

Mawi steps forward. 'But we thought—'

' . . . That I was a monster. But I'm not,' says Novak.

I want to punch her, feed her to the Ropen. I turn to Conner. 'You made me think you were dead.'

He opens his mouth to speak, but the cameraman gets there first. 'You . . . kids thought it was real? I thought it was a joke.'

'You thought pretending to die was a joke?' says Mawi, her lips curling venomously.

'Oh God!' The cameraman looks horrified.

'I'm obviously a better actor than I thought,' says Conner, trying to smile.

'Tell me you're not laughing this off,' I snarl. 'You knew we would believe you were dead.' I catch the expression in Conner's eyes just before he lowers his head. Yeah—he knew! 'We just went into the jungle and nearly died.'

'You would not have died,' says Novak, lifting her hands into the air, as if we're being melodramatic.

'Are you for real?' says Mawi. 'The villagers were going to kill Finn when they saw he'd trapped the Ropen.'

'When Dad hears about this he will not be impressed,' says Blake.

'On the contrary. Your father is over the moon,' says Novak. 'I told him yesterday where you'd been, and he couldn't believe that *you* survived the rainforest. I have to admit I'm rather surprised too.'

'You didn't expect me to come back?'

'No, I knew Finn would bring you back. I just thought you would be in a sorrier state.'

Blake clenches his fists. 'I quit! Your beloved Finn can become Rio.'

Whoa! Where did that come from?

Novak shakes her head. 'You can't. Your contract will not allow it.'

'You think I care about my contract?'

'What if I quit too?' I say.

'Then I pay you nothing, and sue your mama for wasting my time,' says Novak.

'You—' I'm not sure what I want to call her, but the names vanish, as the camera crew return. Truck's with them, and he's carrying a long metal pole with a hook on the end. A bull hook. The sort of medieval device used to train elephants. The sort of thing that should be banned. 'How are you going to direct the Ropen?' I ask.

'I have an animal trainer,' says Novak.

'Truck?'

'Yes,' she says in surprise, until she spots him. 'Ah!'

'I thought he was our minder and tutor.'

234

'He can teach you how to train the Ropen, if you like,' she says, with a twisted smile.

'He can't use that hook on her.'

'He can use whatever will work,' says Novak. She claps her hands. 'Stations, everyone. We need to film this momentous occasion.'

The camera crew rush to their tripods, some climb into the cabs of cranes. Almost every person who works on the film is here. Sound, lighting, runners . . .

It's mad. It's as if we haven't just risked our lives in the jungle. It's as if Novak is a normal director. Not a murderous witch. In a daze I watch them set up. Truck unclips a ring of keys off his belt. He slides one into the padlock dangling from the cage.

'You might want to stand back,' he says to us.

We shuffle backwards, until we hit the trees behind. Truck pushes the hooked end of the long pole in between two bars of the cage door and looks at Novak.

'Cameras ready? Lights ready? Sound ready? Action,' she says.

Using the hook, Truck pulls open the door, then drops the pole. I let out a huge breath I didn't even know I was holding. So *that's* why he has it.

The Ropen watches Truck warily, before limping out. Her left ankle, covered in a metal clasp, drags a thick-coiled chain connected to the floor of the cage. She steps onto the grass and spreads out her wings.

'Truly magnificent,' says Novak, breathlessly.

The Ropen beats her wings, and rises into the air. The chain tightens and yanks at her ankle. She screeches, and flaps her wings harder. The metal clasp rips at her skin, and blood oozes out.

'Her leg,' I cry.

The Ropen's eyes flicker over us all. She snaps her beak and suddenly dives for the nearest cameraman. The chain jerks her back. She swings her arrow-tipped tail.

'Truck—the whistle!' yells Novak.

Truck pulls out a whistle almost identical to the one I took from Swando, and puts it in his mouth. Once again I can't hear anything, but the Ropen's head sways from side to side and a shriek of anguish rips from her throat. This whistle must give off a different sound.

'She hates that noise,' says Novak. 'To her, it's fingers scraping down a blackboard but a thousand times as loud.'

'Then stop it,' I shout.

The Ropen falls to the ground, her body shaking, I want to rugby-tackle Truck, but it would be as useful as wrestling a tree. Thankfully he takes the whistle out of his mouth. The Ropen still trembles. I want to go over to her, stroke her, tell her it's okay, when in less than a second she's back in the air, charging straight for Truck, hissing. Leaping sideways, he shoves the whistle back into his mouth. The Ropen crumples to the floor, and wails in pain. I wait for Truck to stop, but he keeps on blowing.

'You can't do this,' I shout, running forward, when Mawi and Blake haul me back.

'There's nothing we can do. There's too many of them,' hisses Blake in my ear.

I've never felt so helpless in my life, but if I can't help, I can't stay and watch. I turn and walk away, sensing Mawi and Blake beside me. We head to the other side of the hotel, to the cliffs, trying to get out of reach of the creature's screams.

'At least our families are safe,' says Blake.

I look out to sea, in the direction of Gamboi Island. 'Yeah? But at what cost?'

CHAPTER 42

The next morning I finally shower. Even I know I stink too much. I want to see the Ropen—make sure she's okay.

I open the door to the hallway ... well I try to. It doesn't budge. It's jammed. I pull harder, use all my strength, but it's no use. I need hotel maintenance. I grab the phone on my bedside table to call reception, but there's no dial tone. The phone line's dead. Suddenly I realize I didn't see any hotel staff yesterday, just film crew.

'Mawi, Blake,' I shout at the top of my voice.

'Finn, is that you?' yells Mawi.

'I'm locked in!'

'We're all locked in,' shouts Blake. 'Novak doesn't

trust us. She came to see me earlier. She wants to carry on filming, only let us out under guarded supervision.'

'Are you serious?'

'Yes!'

As if in a trance, I stagger back to my bed. How does Novak think she'll get away with this? I mean—he's Blake Saunders. She'll have to release us one day. Does she think she can keep us quiet? Or is she going to—I refuse to let my brain go there.

Then I jump up and hurry over to my window. I can scale a few floors. I swear loudly. It's locked too. My eyes dart around the room, and I grab the base of my bedside table. The lamp and clock fall to the ground, not breaking though. I hurl the table at the glass, but it pings off, landing with a crash. My bedroom door bursts open and a runner appears, a knife in his hands.

'What you doing?' he snarls.

Can I get past him, even though he's armed?

The man's eyes flicker between the window and the broken remains on the floor. 'Never going to happen. The glass is bulletproof. Novak's orders before we came here.'

'Why would she have done that? Did she know this was going to happen?' I ask. Perhaps I should rugby-tackle him . . .

The runner shrugs, slams the door, and I hear the lock turn.

'Finn, are you all right?' calls Mawi.

'Yeah,' I lie.

I perch on the edge of my bed, cold enveloping every inch of my body. After some time, I don't know how long, the door opens again. This time Truck enters the room, carrying a plate of food.

'You need to keep your strength up. You have some great stunts lined up,' he says.

I stare at him. He's talking to me as if nothing's happened, as if I'm not a prisoner in a hotel in the middle of nowhere. He and Novak are completely mad. Forcing my voice to remain calm, I decide to play along.

'When will I be doing my stunts?'

'When we're ready. If you need anything, there are film crew in the hallway,' says Truck, putting my plate on the chest of drawers. 'They'll be here all the time.'

So I'm guarded all the time . . .

✳

For the next few days, all I can think about is—what's going to happen next? I talk to Mawi and Blake through the walls, just to stop myself from going mad, but I'm always aware the crew outside can hear. Truck brings all the meals, and I make sure I eat them. I need to keep my strength up, but not for the reason Novak thinks. I do press-ups, sit-ups, and turn my room into a makeshift gym, doing any exercises I can think of to make sure I stay in shape.

On the third morning, Conner, not Truck, opens the door. He shifts uncomfortably. 'You're wanted in 'wardrobe,' he says.

'I'm doing a stunt?'

'With Blake.'

He escorts me out of my room and I see the backs of Blake and Mawi further along the hallway, flanked by film crew.

'Novak really doesn't trust us,' I say.

'She doesn't want anyone or anything spoiling this film,' says Conner.

We head to hair and make-up, but different girls are doing it this time.

'The old girls are locked in their rooms too,' says Conner. 'So is the AD. Anyone who shows dissent is—'

'Imprisoned?'

Conner shrugs, and I clench my fists so tight, my nails bury into my skin. 'I really wish I hadn't made her take you back on.'

'She would have rehired me at some point. She needed me to, well . . . you know.'

'Pretend to die?'

'That's the one.'

'And pretend to be my friend,' I mutter.

Conner tilts his head. 'I was and am your friend, Kid.'

'Yeah? Then what the hell do you do to your enemies?'

CHAPTER

43

Blake and I are kept separately so we can't talk. We're dressed the same, except I'm given padding that covers almost every part of my body. *What exactly will I be doing?*

We're taken to the set—a small clearing in the jungle, around the corner from the Ropen's cage. Novak's talking on her mobile in Slovenian—so *she* still has a phone. Sound, lighting, runners, Truck, Alistair—they're all there. Mawi sits on a log, arms wrapped round her legs. I wish I could talk to her.

As soon as Novak spots us, she drops her mobile into her bag and smiles warmly. 'And here are my favourite boys,' she says.

Is she for real? I glance at Blake. He's shaking his head.

'I know you haven't seen a script so let me explain the scene,' she says, as if this is just any other ordinary day.

'You locked us—'

'We are not discussing that now,' says Novak, still smiling, waggling her finger at me.

The film crew glare, and I shut up.

'Blake, this is the first time Rio sees the Ropen, so I want you to be in awe of the creature. But I also want you to feel sickened. The tribe have treated her badly. She's cut.'

'But the villagers didn't cut her,' I say. 'They treated her well, like an equal. They loved her. They—'

'Finn, this is a film. Not real. We will add the cuts to her later with special effects,' says Novak, her smile slipping for a second. Then she looks at me warmly again. 'You are not in shot yet. You are needed once we have filmed Blake's face. Then we will have you stroke the Ropen.'

'I'm not sure she's going to let me stroke her.'

'Try,' says Novak. 'Because then you are going to ride her.'

'What?' I yelp.

'He can't,' says Blake.

'Of course he can. She is much more submissive now.' Novak looks around the clearing before saying, 'Places everyone.'

I walk out of shot, feeling like I'm in some sort of

243

alternative dimension where imprisonment is normal. Blake gets into position.

'Lights, camera, action!'

A nervous-looking actor enters the clearing, holding the end of a lead. Then the Ropen creeps in. Her proud strut has gone. She almost crawls across the ground, her legs bent low as if she's a terrified puppy. Blake's jaw drops, horror filling his face. He's not acting because I'm sure my face is exactly the same. The Ropen opens her beak, lowers her neck, and hisses.

'Cut!' shouts Novak. 'Blake, you were marvellous. Finn, you're up.'

The Ropen watches me warily, and she stamps her claw. I get into Rio's position and the filming begins. I rub my fingertips together, and there's a flash of recognition in her eyes. She lifts her beak and places it gently on my head. I stroke her cheek.

'Cut!' shouts Novak. 'That was spectacular. Truck you have done wonders with her.'

I step back and the Ropen lifts her beak. Truck advances and straight away the Ropen hisses, her eyes darting between him and me. Oh no—she thinks we're together. I shake my head; *I'm nothing like him.*

'How did you get her to do that?' whispers Truck.

The Ropen lunges for him. Truck whips the whistle out of his pocket and blows. She screeches, then immediately cowers.

'Without doing that! She responds to kindness.'

I try to stroke her again, but her beak opens. She makes to bite and I leap back. Truck blows the whistle again. Her legs collapse, and she sinks to the ground, ducking her head as if trying to disappear.

'Stop,' I cry.

Whipping the whistle out of his mouth, he snaps, 'You should be thanking me.'

'She's a wild animal. She can't learn.'

'She will,' says Novak, striding towards me. 'And if she doesn't, she'll stay in that cage forever.'

'What?' Out of the corner of my eye, I see Mawi crouching down in the spot Novak was standing.

'We're going to show her off at film premières,' says Novak. 'She's going to be the star attraction.'

'You're keeping her in *that* tiny cage? The one for the mechanical Ropen?'

'I'll let her out if she learns to behave.' Novak turns to the black heap on the floor and sighs. 'All right, we will try again tomorrow. Truck put her back.'

I look for Mawi. She's back on the log. Did I imagine her move?

Novak follows my gaze. 'Mawi, we will film one of your scenes now. Conner, take her to hair and make-up. And Truck, take the boys back to their rooms after you've dealt with the Ropen.'

Truck stands in front of the creature, and lifts the whistle into the air. The Ropen's eyes widen. With his other hand, he grabs hold of the lead and tugs her upwards. The Ropen looks so pitiful as she clambers to her clawed feet.

I stare in horror at the spot where she's been lying. A sharp jagged stone is covered in bright blue, and neon liquid drips from her underbelly.

'She's cut,' I yelp.

'That will teach her not to lie down,' says Truck, with a laugh.

He yanks her lead again and she stumbles across the ground. More droplets of blue splash onto the grass.

Trying to breathe calmly, I follow them down the path back to the cage. No one else does. The Ropen meekly scuttles inside, Truck following behind. He waves the whistle close to her face, and when she cowers, he bends down. I watch him relock the clasp around her ankle. She could peck him now, stab him in the back with her beak, but she's too fearful, and doesn't know she can.

Truck swaggers out of the cage, his eyes brightening when he sees me.

'She's a dumb animal, but going to make me a fortune,' he says, locking the door, clipping the keys back on his belt.

'You shouldn't hurt her.'

He shrugs just as I spot the bull hook lying on the ground. I leap towards it, but my padding slows me down. Truck snatches the hook before my fingers can grab hold.

'And what were you going to do with that?' he snarls.

I spin around, bend low, and kick him in the chest.

246

He throws the hook to the floor and punches. I duck, and his fist sweeps past. I turn to kick again, when his hand wraps around my neck. Standing behind, he lifts me off the floor. I choke. I kick frantically, my foot connecting with the middle of his legs. He buckles but doesn't let go. I claw at his hand.

'Get off him,' cries Blake, charging towards us. He swipes the bull hook off the grass. 'Let him go!'

Truck squeezes tighter. I can't breathe.

'I said let him go!' roars Blake, swinging the hook.

Truck's fingers release me and I collapse to the ground, gasping for breath.

'Don't ever threaten me again, boy,' says Truck. 'You won't be so lucky next time.' He swaggers away, and I've no idea if he was talking to Blake or me.

'He's forgotten to take us back to our rooms,' says Blake dropping the bull hook. 'Is your neck all right?'

'Who cares about my neck?' I croak. 'I have these.' I hold up the large set of keys I swiped from Truck's belt.

CHAPTER 44

'We should get out of here. Release the others from their rooms,' says Blake.

'I'm releasing her first.'

'But—'

'Any idea which one opens the cage?' I say, fingering the keys.

Blake looks in the direction of the hotel and then back at me. Then he scrapes his hands through his hair. 'I've no idea. But she'll attack you.'

'So? I deserve it.'

I choose one randomly, push it into the padlock, and jiggle. Nothing happens. The Ropen claws the ground with her free foot and screeches.

'Shh,' I hiss.

I try more keys, frantically trying to twist them, when at last the cogs turn and the cage door opens.

'I need you to distract her,' I say.

'Why?' says Blake, then his mouth falls into a perfect O. He's seen the clasp around the Ropen's ankle.

Blake claps his hands. While keeping my eyes on the Ropen, I slip inside, closing the door. She glances at me and hisses. Blake starts whooping. The Ropen lifts her head towards him and I drop to my knees and roll beneath her. Peering up, I'm almost blinded by her bright blue underbelly. Droplets of blue trickle to the ground where she's been cut. I want to stroke her, make her feel better, when she jabs at me with her beak.

I roll from side to side, avoiding her lunging head when I land in something sticky and smelly. Ropen poo! Fighting the urge to vomit, I scramble to the side of the cage near her left foot and pull out the keys. Argh! Which one? Her body and trapped wings thrash against the cage, rattling the metal. Someone's going to come any second.

Vaguely aware of Blake clapping even louder, I shove different keys into the lock. Then something scrapes my back, tearing through my skin. I bite back the scream, and turn to see her balancing on one leg. It must have been her talons. Clenching my jaw, I try another key and the clasp falls apart, dropping away from her ankle.

'Open the door!' I shout.

Blake pulls it open, and jumps out the way.

The Ropen tentatively steps forward with her left leg, then shakes her foot. She knows she's free. She takes another step and I'm now hunched directly beneath her. Suddenly my back burns more than ever, as if someone's pouring lemon juice into my blood. I scream in agony, and the Ropen darts out of the cage, startled. She stretches out her wings and soars into the sky. Higher and higher. Nothing stopping her now. She encircles us.

'Get out of here!' I yell.

'Go!' shouts Blake.

It's as if the Ropen understands. She flies further away. I hurtle out of the cage. We have to get out of here before . . .

Screams fill the jungle and footsteps thunder towards us. We're too late. They've seen her in the sky. Gunshots explode and my eyes dart upwards. Thank God—they haven't hit her. She's too far away.

We start to run, almost crashing into Novak, as she hurtles into the clearing. Truck and Alistair by her side.

Novak's face contorts. 'You! You did this?'

There's no point denying it. I nod.

'How could you? After all I did for you?' she screams.

'All you did for me?' I yell. 'You used me. You sent me to a village where I was almost killed.'

Novak waves her head like a Papuan death adder ready to strike. 'You were a nothing,' she hisses. 'I made you into something. Without me, you'd never be a star. But now, you can go back to being a nothing. A failure.'

'He's not a failure. He's an actor,' yells Mawi, careering

into the clearing with Conner following closely behind.

'An actor?' Novak flings back her head and laughs. 'Have you seen him act? He's pathetic. He's got no talent.' Her eyes fall back to me. 'I looked at your audition tape for the Saunders scholarship. How did you win? I've never seen anything so pathetic in my life.' Spit flies from her mouth, landing on my cheek.

My back burns, but that's nothing compared to her words.

'He's great,' says Blake.

'He can do a few tricks, anyone can learn them. But he will never be on film again. I'm not sure he'll even breathe again.' Novak turns to Truck. 'I'm not sure any of the children will breathe again. They can disappear in a horrible accident. Like Anna's. But deadly.'

She hurt Anna on purpose!

Novak points at Blake, her eyes glinting. 'If you die in a stunt, *The Ropen's Revenge* will be remembered forever. There won't be an Oscar, but no one will ever stop talking about this film.'

Just how mad is she?!

'We could give them high doses of sleeping medicine in their hot chocolate,' says Conner. 'It doesn't have to hurt.'

They must have drugged us the night everyone disappeared!

'We need something more dramatic. How about fire?' says Truck.

I feel like my brain is exploding. They're talking about our deaths as if they're brainstorming ideas for a film. Not real life. I glance at Alistair. At least he has the decency to look frightened too.

Should we run for it? Head for the rainforest? I turn to Mawi and Blake, hoping they can read my mind.

It seems that Novak is the mind-reader. 'Of course, we could just let you go. None of you would survive the jungle. We're too far away from any civilization.' She steps even closer to me. 'You shouldn't have let the Ropen go, Finn. You didn't want to make me mad.'

'You were never going to let us live.' I say.

She smiles coldly. 'Take them back to their rooms while I think of an interesting accident.'

Truck moves towards us, when suddenly there's a throb of rotor blades.

CHAPTER
45

Police sirens wail over the rainforest. Our faces dart skyward as five helicopters roar into view.

'Nobody move!' shouts a voice over a megaphone. 'Put your hands in the air or we will fire.'

Our arms shoot up.

I can hardly believe my eyes as ropes drop from the aircrafts. Police slide down, landing on the ground, their guns pointing at us.

'Novak, you're under arrest,' shouts a policeman.

'Who called you?' she demands.

'I did,' says Mawi, and she waves Novak's mobile in the air.

I want to hug her! She must have taken it when I saw

her move off the log.

'That's my phone,' shrieks Novak. 'She's a thief. You should arrest her.'

'If she's right about what you've been up to, I think a stolen phone is the least of your worries,' says the policeman.

Novak twists around to face Conner. 'You were supposed to guard her.'

'She wanted the toilet. Was I supposed to watch her wee?'

'Yes!' she yells, and starts to run.

A gunshot fires in the air.

'Next time, we will aim for you,' shouts the policeman.

Novak freezes, and he snaps handcuffs around her wrists. More policemen head for Truck, Alistair, and . . .

Pain explodes across my back, like millions of adders biting at the same time. My legs crumple and I collapse to the floor.

'What's wrong with him?' cries the first policeman.

'The Ropen scratched his back,' says Blake.

Mawi's voice sounds distant: 'There's blue stuff in his cut.'

The policeman sweeps me over his shoulder and I black out.

*

The next few days pass in a haze, possibly due to my diet of painkillers and sleeping tablets. The doctor stitched

254

up my back at some point. She wanted to take me to the hospital in Port Moresby but the AD refused. They're trying to keep news of the Ropen quiet. All the film crew who were against Novak have been released from their rooms. The police want to talk to us, but we can do that back in England. I learn all this from Mawi and Blake who visit me as soon as they can.

'Mawi, you were incredible. You stole Novak's mobile—that was inspired,' I say. 'You saved us.'

Her face breaks into a massive grin. 'But it was you who released the Ropen.'

'How is she? Do either of you know?'

'She's back at Gamboi Island. The police checked with Swando's dad,' says Blake.

'They know Swando's father?'

'Apparently the Chief of Police has known him for years, and known about the Ropen too. They don't let news of her get out in case the press or scientists hound her. They had no idea Novak was trying to find a real Ropen. They thought she was using the mechanical one or CGI.'

'To be fair, that's what we all thought.' I pause. 'Does that mean Swando's father is okay?'

'He's a lot better,' says Mawi. 'And the police explained why we caught her, so hopefully Swando can forgive us.'

I hope so, but I doubt it.

Mawi sits on the end of my bed. 'All footage of the Ropen's been destroyed. If anyone mentions her, their sentences are going to be doubled. Novak, Truck, Conner, Alistair, and loads of others—they were all arrested.'

'There's been a massive buzz in the news about why the film was stopped,' says Blake. 'So the AD told the press Novak was an absolute nightmare to work with. And he has funds, so is making sure everyone's looked after financially. He feels dreadful this happened—that he didn't spot what she was planning to do, what she was capable of. None of us are allowed to talk about the Ropen though.' He pauses. 'We're going home tomorrow. The AD's been waiting until you're well enough to travel.'

'We are?' My eyes dart to Mawi.

She bites her lip. 'Actually, I'm going home today.'

'That sucks,' I whisper.

'I know, but my parents say I can wave you off at the airport.'

'That's good.'

Her eyes grow wet all of a sudden. 'I've got to go.'

Before I can say anything, she darts out of the room.

'What was that abou—' My words vanish as I stare at the thing flying through the open window. Because it is a thing—the size of a mouse, with the head of a lion, the body of a winged horse. It lands on my left leg, and I scoot backwards. My stitches burn, as they scrape against the bed board.

'Can you see it?' I yelp.

'What's happened to your eyes?' says Blake.

The creature tilts its head, looks directly at me, then flies back out the window.

'Did you see that?' I say, louder this time.

'They're bright blue,' says Blake.

'They are blue,' I say, distractedly, not taking my eyes off the window.

'Yeah, but they're not brighter than mine,' he says. 'Oh! They're back to normal now'

I'm vaguely aware of Blake still muttering about eye colour. What was that thing? Then I spot the medicine packet on the top of the bedside cabinet, and I almost laugh out loud. Of course—the painkillers are making me hallucinate.

CHAPTER

46

I don't see any more mini-lion horses that night or the next morning, possibly because I stop taking the painkillers. My back hurts, but I'd rather have pain than lose my mind. I'm not looking forward to the plane ride home. Without Novak paying, I'm sure I'll be in economy. Not that I mind being in the cheap seats—any plane ride will be amazing—but it's the hours I'll have to endure with my back against an upright seat that bothers me.

The runway in Port Moresby is empty; no press or dignitaries. Only those working on the film, heading for home, stand on the tarmac. The AD wants us to slip away quietly. I glance around for about the hundredth time.

'She'll be here,' says Blake. 'She'll want to say goodbye.'

'Don't you want to say goodbye too?'

'Not as much as you,' he says, shoving me.

Then I spot her, walking toward us flanked by an older man and woman.

'Blake, Finn, these are my parents,' calls Mawi, waving her arm in the air.

As soon as they reach us, her mum says, 'It is so good to meet you. We've heard so much about you.'

'You're all she's been talking about.'

'Dad!' says Mawi, looking mortified.

Blake steps forward, and I stay where I am.

'You're Finn, aren't you?' says Mawi's father, holding out his hand to me. Blake's jaw drops, and I can't help but grin. *Mawi's been talking about me!* 'Yeah—I'm Finn.'

'Well thank you so much for looking after our daughter,' he says.

Blushing, Mawi grabs onto my arm and Blake's too. 'Come on,' she says, dragging us away to an empty spot on the runway.

'Parents are put on this planet to embarrass us,' I say, and she smiles gratefully.

'So? You've been talking about Finn, have you?' says Blake, folding his arms, but grinning at the same time. 'I think you've forgotten that I'm the real Rio. He's not good-looking enough.'

Suddenly Mawi leans forward and kisses me on the lips. My brain freezes. By the time I work out I have to respond, she's moved back, her cheeks flaming even more.

'I'll miss you,' she says, quickly turning away, walking back to her parents.

'You should probably close your mouth,' says Blake.

'She kissed me. Really kissed me.'

'Yeah, we saw.'

'Should I do something?'

'Not with her parents watching,' says Blake.

I turn to see them looking at me not quite as warmly as before. In fact everyone is staring, most are grinning, others are trying not to laugh. Heat races up my neck, my face, my ears.

'Oh great! My first kiss was in front of the crew,' I mutter.

'Not as bad as mine. My first kiss was in front of the director and my dad who continued to shout instructions all the way through.'

I burst out laughing. 'Yeah—you win.' Then I see Mawi staring, and she looks hurt. Does she think I was laughing at her? Suddenly I don't care that everyone is watching. 'I'll miss you too,' I yell.

Her face lights up. 'Will you write?'

'I'll write, text, and call.'

'Okay, this is getting far too soppy now,' says Blake. 'We've got to go.'

There are two staircases leading to the plane, one towards the front, the other at the back. I start to head for the one at the back, when Blake grabs my arm. 'Where are you going?'

'To my seat.'

'You're in First Class.'

'Not without Novak paying. I'll be with the rest of the crew in economy.'

'I got Dad to upgrade you.'

'You did?'

'Yeah. Think of it as a thank you.'

'For what?'

'Saving my life.'

*

An hour later, we're up in the sky. I'm lying on my stomach in a soft reclining seat. 'Thanks for this,' I say.

'Not a problem,' says Blake.

'And . . . and I'm sorry about the advert. You know—the one back in England.'

Blake shakes his head. 'Don't bring that up now, not when I'm beginning to like you again.'

'But I want you to know I didn't have a choice. I—'

'Finn, it's fine, I get it,' says Blake. 'Anyway, I've got something far more interesting to tell you. I spoke to Dad this morning. I said that I'd only be in the next Rio film, if you could be my stunt double. The AD has already found a new director for it.'

'Are you serious?' I say, sitting up.

Blake nods. 'It's so much better having you than a girl do my stunts.'

'But according to Novak I can't act.'

261

Blake looks me straight in the eyes. 'Listen, I'm only going to say this once. You are a great stunt double. You do anything. You're way better than professionals twice your age.'

I swallow and nod. I can't seem to find the words.

'But you're a rubbish straight actor. God knows why Dad gave you that scholarship.'

I smile. Same old Blake.

'And don't think for one minute I'm going to be nice to you on set. You're still going to have to be my slave— sorry, I mean PA.'

'Ah, the real reason you want me.'

'Would there be any other?'

I hesitate. 'I don't suppose I could ask you for a favour?'

'Another one? I've already got you into a film. What more do you want?'

'Your autograph. But not for me,' I add quickly. 'The girls at school were pestering me.'

Blake's face breaks into a giant grin. 'Oh stop lying. I know you want it for your bedroom wall.'

After Blake signs pieces of paper with each of the girls' names attached (they're going to love me for this) I drift off to sleep. I think the tablets are still running through me because I don't wake up until we're nearly back in London. It's obvious Blake's been busy. He's now wearing clean jeans and a fleece, and his hair is perfectly gelled. Glancing at my reflection in the window, I snort out loud. I have bed hair and drool. No one would mistake me for Rio now.

Following Blake, I step off the plane into a long metal tube that takes us back inside Heathrow airport. We're swept though security before heading to Arrivals where the crowds are enormous. Straight away cameras flash for Blake. The paparazzi swarm around him, pushing me out the way. I don't mind. There's only one person I want to see.

I look about and there she is. Alive and well.

'Mum!' I shout, rushing over, wrapping my arms around her.

She steps back looking surprised. Then smiles and cuddles me too. I don't care who sees us, but no one's paying us the slightest attention. They're watching the reunion between Blake and his family.

'I can't believe they're cancelling the entire film,' says Mum.

'They're going to do another Rio film though, with a different director.'

'But they won't let you be a stunt double, will they?'

'Actually they will. Blake's made sure of it.'

'Blake? Are you friends again?'

'Yeah, I think we are.'

Mum beams, when something the size of a donkey streaks across the room behind her, disappearing around the corner. My heart starts pounding. Was that a dragon? I look around to see if anyone else has noticed, but no one seems shocked or terrified. There are no screams coming from where it went.

Then I glance back at Mum. She's staring at me like I've turned into a dragon.

'Your eyes!' she exclaims. 'They're bright blue.'

'What is it with you and Blake going on about my eyes?'

'They're flashing neon, like you've got some dye in them.'

My heart pounds even more. Mawi's words fill my brain.

'My great-uncle used to talk about it all the time. He believed that anyone who came in contact with the Ropen would get haunted by the spirit world. Mythological beasts would find you, feed off your energy.'

Oh God.

That can't be true.

Can it?

ABOUT THE AUTHOR

Tamsin loves to travel, have adventures, and see wild animals. She's fed a tiger, held a seven-foot python, and stroked a tarantula, but she's too scared to touch a worm. She lives in Somerset with her adrenalin-junkie family, and likes to think her Nahualli (spirit animal) would be a jaguar or a lioness. Her friends tell her it's a Labradoodle!

GLOSSARY OF FILM TERMS

ASSISTANT DIRECTOR (AD): The AD assists the Director in making sure the film is actually shot and the production stays on schedule. (Normally there are three ADs for each film, but to stop confusion, I have cast only one Assistant Director in Stunt Double.)

BOOM: A Boom is a long, movable pole that has a microphone or camera on one end.

CLAPPERBOARD: A Clapperboard is used in filmmaking to mark particular scenes and takes recorded during a production. Also it helps synchronize picture and sound.

DIRECTOR: A Director is the person who directs the making of a film. They have a vision for the script and drama, and guide the crew and actors to fulfil it.

EXTRA: An Extra is a performer in a film, who appears in a non-speaking capacity, usually in the background, such as in a busy street scene.

JIB: A Jib operates a bit like a see-saw, using counterweights to balance the camera. It allows for camera movements and camera angles that you couldn't otherwise achieve.

ON LOCATION: This is when the movie is filmed in an actual setting rather than in a studio.

PRODUCER: Producers plan and coordinate various aspects of film production, such as selecting script, coordinating writing, directing and editing, and arranging financing.

RUNNER: A Runner is the most junior role. They make cups of tea, photocopy scripts, find people, etc… Basically they do what anyone asks them to.

STUNT COORDINATOR: A Stunt Coordinator is an experienced stunt performer. They design, choreograph, and organize the stunt scene, working closely with the Director. They make sure the stunts look real while maintaining safety for all those involved. Normally they are involved in casting. (Obviously Alistair wasn't!)

STUNT DOUBLE: A Stunt Double is a type of body double who is properly trained to perform dangerous stunt sequences. They are used if a main actor is not physically able or contractually allowed to perform stunts. (Blake likes to say it's because he isn't allowed. Or do you think he just didn't want to?)

STUNT PERFORMER: A Stunt Performer—often referred to as a stuntman, stuntwoman, or daredevil—is someone who performs dangerous stunts, often as a career. Highly trained, they can be in car crashes and explosions. They can fall from great heights or be dragged behind a horse. They must follow the Stunt Coordinator's direction. (I don't think Finn read this!)

TAKE: A Take is a single continuous recorded performance. The term is used to track the stages of production.

TUTOR: A Tutor makes sure child actors keep their schoolwork up to date while on location. (I don't think Truck read this either!)

INTERVIEW WITH TAMSIN COOKE

1) WHERE DID THE IDEA COME FROM FOR THIS BOOK?

I was watching my fourteen-year-old son Free Running. He was climbing, jumping, tumbling from great heights, and he reminded me of a stuntman. It occurred to me that being a stunt double would be the perfect job for a teenager – full of risks, excitement, and glamour. Suddenly I wanted to write about a boy who fell into this world.

2) HOW DID YOU RESEARCH THE STORY?

I had fascinating interviews over tea and cake with a stuntwoman and a film producer. I talked to Extras about their time on set, and I visited Warner Brothers Studio Tour. Even though I haven't been to Papua New Guinea itself, I drew on my time spent in rainforests in Hawaii, Mexico, St Lucia, and Thailand. I watched numerous programmes on Papua New Guinea and became captivated with the country. I also went to the library and scoured the Internet for mythological creatures. It's been great fun and incredibly informative.

3) WHAT HAVE YOU ENJOYED MOST ABOUT WORKING ON THIS BOOK?

I got to interview a real life stuntwoman, Annabel Canaven—who might just be one of the coolest people I have ever met. She gave me such insight into the world of stunts and film. She showed me video footage of being set on fire and falling backwards off a cliff. There's a part of me that would love to have her job. Then the bigger part of me remembers I'm not brave. I'll write about it instead!

4) WHY DID YOU DECIDE TO INCLUDE A ROPEN INTO THE STORY?

I wanted a relatively unknown creature that possibly existed in a remote part of the world. There have been reported sightings of the Ropen in Papua New Guinea, making her the perfect choice.

5) WHAT INTRIGUED YOU ABOUT THE WORLD OF MOVIE-MAKING, PARTICULARLY THE ROLE OF STUNT DOUBLE?

I'm amazed at the number of people it takes to make a film. Often it's only the actors, the director, and possibly the producer that we know of. The rest of the large film crew are unsung heroes, especially stunt doubles who put their lives on the line without getting much credit.

6) WHAT WERE YOUR FAVOURITE MOVIES GROWING UP?

Ooh, I had so many. Mary Poppins, ET (which still makes me cry), The Dark Crystal, Annie, The Karate Kid, Pretty in Pink, The Slipper and the Rose. Goodness—I could go on and on … I loved all sorts of films and still do. It doesn't matter whether they're massive sweeping adventures, musicals, comedy, or thrillers. You name it—if it's a good story, I'll enjoy it.

7) DID ANY FILMS DIRECTLY INSPIRE THIS STORY?

I loved the pterodactyls swooping over the park in Jurassic World. They were the perfect mixture of power and grace and gave me lots of inspiration for the Ropen. There's also a TV series from the 80s called The Fall Guy which I used to watch when I was younger. It's about a Hollywood stuntman, who used all his skills and knowledge of stunts and special effects to capture criminals.

8) WHAT IS THE MOST INTERESTING FACT THAT YOU DISCOVERED WHEN RESEARCHING THE STORY?

I had no idea that women performed the stunts of teenage boys. It makes a lot of sense since anyone under the age of eighteen isn't allowed to do the risky scenes, and full-blown stuntmen are often too tall or muscly.

ACKNOWLEDGEMENTS

I have so many 'thank yous' to give to so many amazing people that I decided to write my acknowledgements as if this were an Oscar speech. Finn has already written his, although he wouldn't admit it to anyone.

So here goes:

Thank you, thank you to everyone who has helped me make this book a reality. (I clutch the trophy to my chest and gaze adoringly at the audience.) None of this would have been possible but for my agent, Anne Clark. Not only has she shown unwavering support, she's answered my neurotic emails and telephone calls. Everyone at OUP has been incredible, particularly my editors, Elv Moody and Gill Sore. They've made sure Stunt Double is the best it can possibly be. Special mention must also go to Lizzie Smart for creating such a fabulously shiny book cover. The blue even matches the new colour scheme in my kitchen.

I cannot adequately express how much I appreciate my family's support. (I wipe tears from the corner of my eyes.) My children, Toby and Daisy, with their sense of fun, adventure, and risk-taking are the inspiration behind the story. My husband Graham's advice, humour, and amazing cooking have kept me sane and alive! I'd like to thank my dad who is always so proud and happy when I share the slightest bit of book news. And I'd like to thank my sister, Pia, who helps me unlock my creativity as well as always being there for me.

Two people need a special mention. I'm incredibly grateful to Annabel Canaven, a professional stuntwoman, who gave me great insight into the world of stunt performers. I'm in awe of her life—throwing herself through glass, off cliffs, and getting set on fire. Also I want to thank Rory Calver, a Film Producer, who told me so much about movie making. If any of this book is incorrect, please don't blame either one of these wonderful people. I may have taken artistic licence!

Many great friends and family members have been enthusiastic about my creative journey. In particular, Sophie, Helen, Charlotte and Nic have been great at listening to my new story ideas and offering fabulous advice. Unfortunately I don't have the time to name everyone, but I hope you know who you are. Thank you dearly for your support.

My last thank you goes out to all the readers of Stunt Double. I hope you enjoyed reading about Finn's adventures as much as I enjoyed writing them.

(Waving the trophy in the air, I walk off stage, desperately hoping I don't trip up!)

TURN OVER
FOR A TASTE
OF FINN'S NEXT
EXCITING
ADVENTURE...

Why did I say I'd do this? I must be out of my mind!

'Take a deep breath!' shouts a voice.

I inhale sharply, sensing rather than seeing the fiery torch approach. I hear a whoosh, and know I've been lit. The flames must be blazing down my back, over my legs. It's weird there's no heat. The fire's building. It's rumbling louder than a high-speed train. I'm supposed to do something. But what? My brain has frozen as if it can't believe I'm alight.

Then instinct kicks in.

I lurch towards fresh air, away from the smoke. I pump my arms and see they're covered in bright orange flames. I stumble faster as if I can outrun my limbs. Fire spreads to my stomach. I want to breathe, but I can't. It'll scorch my lungs.

Suddenly I feel heat seep into the back of my knee, and remember my training. I bellyflop to the ground as if shot in the back. Fire extinguishers explode from all directions. A blanket's thrown over me.

I lie still.

'You did it,' yells Seb, my instructor. 'You were a human torch.'

At last I dare to breathe. 'Tell me you got that on film,' I croak, clambering to my feet.

A cameraman grins from behind a tripod. 'Oh no. I forgot to press record.'

'Ha!'

'Are you all right or did you get burnt?' says Seb.

'I felt some heat behind my knee. That's why I dropped to the ground.'

'Good, you've learnt well,' he says, throwing me a tube of cream. 'After your shower, rub that into the places that hurt. Right, Emma, you're up next ... ' He turns away, already setting the next trainee up for their brush with fire.

I head for the washroom. I can't believe I just did that. But actually, out of all the stunts I've done over the last two weeks, being set on fire was the easiest. I didn't really have to do anything. I just needed a team who made sure I was prepared and put the flames out afterwards. It's not like learning to fight with swords or rolling down spiral staircases.

I yank off the gloves, my hood, and the many outer layers of clothes. Then I peel off the fire-retardant long underwear. I can't wait to get in the shower. My face and hair are covered in special cooling gel, and I bet I look like a blob fish. At least I had all this protective gear, though. If I'd been on set for *The Ropen's Revenge*, the director would have asked me to do the stunt without any special clothing. The worst thing is—I would have said yes.

Half an hour later, I'm dressed in the course uniform of shorts and t-shirt with the *British Legion of Stunt Performers* logo stamped across the front. Returning to the common room, I find the rest of my course. They're at least four years older than me.

'All right everyone, gather around,' says Seb, as soon as I step inside. 'First of all I'd like to say a huge well done. Getting set on fire is a leap of faith. And you all passed this section. But what you didn't know—is that my colleagues and I were timing you. We wanted to see which one of you could stay standing the longest, while set alight. The winner gets to come in late tomorrow. The rest of you have to run three miles before breakfast.'

'You could have warned us,' says Emma.

'And have some of you burnt to a crisp just to win? I don't think so.'

I glance around the room, my eyes falling on Callum. He's only a bit taller than me, but I think his idea of fun is weightlifting buses. And for some reason he thinks he's God's gift to the planet. Just let me have lasted longer than him.

Seb looks down at his clipboard. 'Starting with the shortest amount of time. We have . . . Finn Gibson.'

I was last???

Callum sniggers.

I cross my fingers. *Call his name next . . .*

'Then we have Simon.'

Argh!

He runs through sixteen more names until only two are left.

'Emma, you did incredibly well with two minutes forty-eight seconds. But Callum beat you with three minutes seventeen.'

Just great!

Strutting to the front, like he's some sort of 'heavy' from a gangster film, Callum says, 'I guess I'm made of stronger stuff than the others.' He pumps his arms and I half expect him to kiss his biceps.

Vomiting sounds come from around the room, and no one claps.

'Okay everyone, we're done for the day,' says Seb. 'But I just want to add: None of you should try this stunt at home to get a longer time. That includes you, Finn.'

'I'm not stupid,' I say.

'You're a fourteen-year-old boy. Of course you're stupid. Well . . . you have stupid ideas. Promise me, you won't do this again without a stunt team present.'

'I promise,' I mumble.

'I don't even know why he's here. He's not old enough,' says Callum.

Seb sighs. 'Like I've told you many times, Finn has got special permission.'

'He's slowing the course down.'

'Enough!' says Seb.

'He always needs extra help.'

That's it. I'm fed up with being quiet. 'I needed extra help one time because I've never driven a car before,' I snap. 'Tell me Callum, exactly how many stunts have you performed on film? And not just during this course so you can get a tick in the box. I mean on actual movie sets?'

Callum grimaces. 'I don't know how you got work. You're the worst here. Just scraping by.'

'I said enough!' shouts Seb. 'Callum, you've lost your late start. All of you, go home.'

I hurtle out the door before the others, and storm along the corridor, taking a left at the end. When my new director told me I was going on this course, I'd been looking forward to it so much, but now . . .

God I hate Callum. I wish he'd—

I freeze.

Sitting in the middle of the floor is a small hairless dog with fangs dripping down and a forked tail. It looks like a devil dog! This is the first time I've seen a strange creature since back at the airport where I thought I saw a dragon.

No, I'm not going there. Must have been jet lag.

The dog tilts its head and wags its tail. I'm sure it's someone's designer pooch. I step towards it, when it bares its teeth and its eyes glare red . . . It really is a devil dog. My heart thunders in my ears. The dog leaps to its feet and charges straight for me. I twist and run. At the end I take a left instead of a right and suddenly I'm facing a dead end with a closed door.

Please don't be locked.

I grab the handle and almost scream with relief when it opens. I slam the door shut, just as claws scrape against it. A snarling snout pokes through the gap between the door and the floor.

I shuffle backwards, realising I'm in the fighting room. Cabinets filled with swords, daggers, and nunchucks line the walls. I could grab a weapon if I have to.

The door handle begins to turn. Since when can dogs do that? I dart behind the nearest cabinet and peer out.

What the—?

Blake's mum and dad stand in the doorway. I'm a stunt double for Blake, but I haven't seen his mother for years. She hates me; thinks I'm too poor and common to hang out with her precious son. His dad's all right. But the pair of them are Hollywood royalty. They have seven Oscars between them. So what the hell are they doing in this stunt school?

Then I hear a snarl. You're kidding me? Devil dog's reappeared, weaving in and out of their legs. Can't they see it? They're not reacting to it at all.

'Why have you dragged me in here?' It's Marcus, Blake's dad.

'Before we go another step, I want you to promise me no one knows about this,' says Blake's mum. Even though her voice is hushed and urgent, she still manages to sound cold and haughty.

'Of course no one knows.'

She tuts. 'I don't see why we had to come to this . . . this place.'

'I want to see how he's getting on.'

'It's reckless. Have you thought about what it looks like? People will start asking questions.'

'No one knows I'm here for Finn,' says Marcus. 'They think I'm checking out the school.'

I lean against the cabinet. *He's here for me?*

She pulls a face. 'You know I don't like them being together. Blake and Finn should be kept apart.'

I snort silently. She's still a snob.

Then her voice gets louder. 'What if Blake finds out?'

'He won't,' says Marcus. 'Finn has no idea I'm his father. So how could he possibly tell Blake?'

His words ricochet off the walls. The world tilts and my legs crumple. I don't even notice devil dog running straight for me.